DEEP DARKNESS

A novel by

A. A. Akibibi

A. A. Akibibi

ISBN: 979-8-9856812-1-5
979-8-9856812-2-2

ACKNOWLEDGEMENTS

Isabel Lieb, I can't thank you enough for your amazing cover designs. Thanks to my family, for encouraging me in my writing. And thanks to the staff and students I work with, and the opportunity I have to learn and grow with them.

Yuayua Publishing
Le Center, MN

CONTENTS

A. A. Akibibi

CHAPTER 1

Inspiration

This is the greatest feeling ever! I have always dreamed of winning the World Stratagem Finals. It's surreal to be here now, holding the huge golden trophy in my hands. The faces of Mom, Hilda, and Bo are beaming up at me from the crowd. Hoss is standing to my right, shouting 'yeah!', his eyes blazing with joy as he hoists a silver trophy over his head in triumph.

Looking down past Mom and Bo, I realize that we are standing in Dead Man's Theater – the balcony of an abandoned building we watch Stratagem games from. Beads of sweat form across my brow. The sun feels like a blow-torch against my cheek. Only a few tattered shreds are left of the balcony awning, and they don't give any shade. The balcony creaks every time someone shifts his feet. There have never been so many people up on Dead Man's Theater. How long before it collapses under all the added weight? It's so bizarre that the World Stratagem Finals would be held here, at the vacant lot in Victoria.

An instant later, we are all standing outside Trayman's Ice Cream Shoppe celebrating with sundaes. Waph has joined us, his watery blue-gray eyes bright with laughter. The cool treat feels good as it slides down my throat. I'm eating barbequed mint chocolate ice cream with garlic sauce…

My eyes snap open to a rainbow of color. I wistfully snatch at the images, trying to hold them clearly in my mind. But even now, the last traces of the dream are slipping away.

Reality is harsh. I'm still here on the *Aurora*, the scientific exploration vessel my dad works on. We're still in this weird region of space, where light is a rainbow of colors, gravity is weird, and there are tulip-shaped aliens that live in orbit around their planet. Bo, Hoss, and Hilda are back on Earth, in some other reality, impossibly far away. And Mom. Mom is dead. I will never see her again. Or hear her cheerful laugh.

I climb dully to my feet and prepare to meet another day of drudgery. As I exit my cabin, I think about how crazy the universe is. Take time, for example. It's such a curious thing. During history lessons, seconds plod along like an old, weary horse. But in a game of Stratagem, hours flit by, as if they are plunging recklessly down an icy mountain.

Right now, time seems to barely move at all. I am waiting anxiously for things to get back to normal – like light and gravity – so that we can return to Earth. It should have happened by now. I'm sure of it. We left the tulip people's planet over a week ago. It didn't take us this long to get there. Which means we are either heading in the wrong direction – which wouldn't surprise me at all – or there *isn't* a way to get back home. This thought is too depressing. I choose not to believe it; there *has* to be a way back.

I flop down on a couch in the lounge and look out the viewport. Tiny ribbons of rainbow-colored light stream past outside, like sparkles in a vast black jewel. I watch, mesmerized, as I think about all the things that have happened since joining my dad on the *Aurora*.

I suddenly remember that Mr. Dunberger, the person who dropped me off on the *Aurora*, wants to hear about my trip when we get back... if we ever get back (don't say that! I scold myself. We are getting back!). I decide to make notes, so that when we *do* get back, I'll be able to tell him about my adventures without forgetting anything. I pull out my graphic pad and get started.

Light, gravity, the *Aurora's* shields, asteroid collisions, working with Roberts, Wiggs's weird recipes, the contaminated water, iridium, the tulip people – I detail each one. It takes me about ten minutes to finish the notes. I stop, read back through what I've written, and reword a few lines. Satisfied, I am just about to return the graphic pad to my pocket when I hear the lounge door whoosh open.

"Hi Waph," I say, after glancing up to see who's entering. He was in the dream…

"Oh, hi Sean," he replies, bringing my thoughts to a halt. "Mind if I sit here for a bit?"

"Not at all," I say, surprised that he's even asking. There are some adults who would probably try to kick me out if they were coming in here.

"What're you working on?" Waph asks, settling on a seat beside me.

"Remember Mr. Dunberger, the guy who brought me to the *Aurora*?"

"Dark suit, black hat?" Waph asks.

"That's him," I say, my mind flashing back to the way Mr. D holds his hat in his hands, and the way he nibbles his food.

I firmly put these images out of my mind; it's too depressing to think about him. Doing so reminds me of Mom's death, and leaving my friends, and leaving Earth. Instead, I continue, "He told me he wants to hear about our trip when we get back. I'm just writing stuff down so that I remember everything."

"That's a good idea," Waph says, smiling. I wish I could see his blue eyes clearly in this light. I like the way they sparkle when he smiles. "Why don't you run it by me; see if you've missed anything."

I think about this for a moment. I'm pretty sure I've remembered everything, but it wouldn't hurt to get his input.

"Sure," I say. I start reading him my notes about the weird light and gravity.

"Hold on a moment," Waph says, before I've gotten more than three lines into the notes. I look up, a bit miffed that he's interrupting me. "Why don't you write it as a play?"

I snort in surprise. "A play? I wouldn't have the slightest idea how to write a play. And I doubt Mr. D would care for it very much."

"It would just be for fun," Waph says. "Think of a role for each of us." He must see my puzzled look, because he hurries on. "For example, Sharden and the captain could be tulip people."

This leaves me even more confused. The captain and Sharden are the last people I could ever picture playing tulip people. They would make a complete mess of it!

"Of course first," Waph adds, "We would have to find them some nice dainty costumes."

This thought makes me burst out laughing. "You mean all pink and frilly?" I manage to choke out, picturing the pair of them in tutus and tiaras.

"Absolutely," Waph agrees. "Now you're getting the idea. And Wiggs could be the asteroids."

I nod. Now that I understand what he means, the thoughts start flowing. "Roberts would play the part of our voices changing," I say, picturing the crazy-eyed scientist speaking in a deep bass voice, then sucking in some helium and speaking in a squeaky voice. "And my dad could do some daring wirework to show the reversed gravity."

"Marcum would definitely need to be the rainbow colors," Waph adds. "And he would need more than just a costume. We would need paint for his face and hands as well."

Picturing the stern engineer dancing onto stage in a rainbow-colored leotard and face paint makes me chuckle again. This is fun!

We work on the play together – the crew of the *Aurora*, acting out the events we have experienced. We find the perfect part for each of us, although some have to take on multiple roles (we've assigned five to Sharden and Roberts, and four to the captain). We reach the point where Kartak gets violently sick from eating the tulip people's food.

"And that's it so far," I say, making a couple more notes before stowing the graphic pad in my pocket. "I just hope I get a chance to share it with Mr. D someday. He would love it!"

"We'll make it back," Waph says firmly. I'm not sure if he's saying this to try to reassure me, or because he truly believes it.

"I know we will," I say, although without a whole lot of confidence.

My stomach rumbles. This isn't surprising; we really have to ration our food just to survive. These days, I have a constant pain in my stomach from hunger. I look forward to my meals with Wiggs more than ever – even though he gets ingredients mixed up, making the food taste strange, with him I always leave feeling *almost* full.

"Computer, what time is it?" I ask.

"It is seven minutes past one," the computer replies promptly. I groan. We have almost five more hours until supper. I'm so hungry, my stomach might start gnawing on itself by then.

"Anxious for supper?" Waph asks, correctly interpreting my reaction.

"I'm starving," I say, rubbing my tummy, trying to ease some of the ache.

"Yeah, we're all feeling the pinch," Waph says. "I haven't had a decent meal since we celebrated Kartak's recovery…" The scientist's voice trails off, so that I can hardly hear the last word. His face turns thoughtful for a moment, and then his eyes grow wide. "That's it!" he exclaims. "Hydroponics!"

Waph pops to his feet and rushes from the room, leaving me in confused silence. Hydroponics? What's that going to solve? One thing is for sure; I'm not going to find out by sitting here.

Jumping up from the couch, I hurry after Waph to discover what he's so excited about. The lounge door slides open. I look both ways. The corridor is empty. Waph must have turned left, otherwise he would probably still be in sight. This means he isn't going to hydroponics. My curiosity deepens.

I head left. The wishbone junction presents another choice. Where would Waph be going? If he's going to see the captain, the bridge makes sense, and it's closest. I decide to check there first.

As soon as the hatch opens, I know my guess is correct. I can hear Waph's excited voice babbling about spare parts and pipes.

"What do you think?" the captain asks Kartak sharply.

Another scientist replies, sounding thoughtful. "I think we should be able to jury-rig something. It'll put a strain on our water supply, though."

"Yes. It's a good thing we got some water from those flowery aliens," the captain says. "Otherwise, there wouldn't be any chance of making this work. I want the two of you to check into the possibility right away!"

"Yes, sir!" Waph says.

"As you wish," says Kartak, almost at the same time.

I still don't know what it's about. What are they going to jury-rig? Why would it put a strain on our water supply?

Then the answer hits me. It's so obvious, I'm shocked that no one has thought of it before. They are going to try creating more hydroponics vats! Right now we can grow enough food for three, maybe four people. After all, our hydroponics was designed to supplement the regular rations with fresh fruits and vegetables, not to provide entire meals. If we're able to expand hydroponics, we wouldn't have to ration our food quite so much.

I'm so excited at this thought, I want to race after Waph and Kartak and be the first to know whether we have the materials to make it work. Still, I don't want to be a nuisance. Perhaps I can watch from a distance.

I follow them down to the holds, and wait at each hatch as they inventory items that might be cobbled together to make hydroponics vats. I'm no expert, so I have no idea what to make of the parts they are finding; still, the excitement in their voices is encouraging.

After searching the holds, they run over the list they've made, discussing the various functions the vats will require, and the parts they've found to fit the tasks.

At last, Kartak straightens up. "You know, I think it will work," he says, patting Waph on the back. "Great thinking! Let's go tell the captain."

A feeling of great excitement explodes inside me. I'm not sure how many vats they will be able to make, but our food problem might soon be over!

As if to dampen my spirits, my stomach gives a particularly fierce growl; I double over with pain. It feels terrible. What can I do to make it stop?

I consider going to hydroponics to sneak a tomato, but I know it won't do me any good. I was just there this morning, and unless I want to eat an unripe tomato, there won't be anything there for me to pick. I will simply have to suffer until suppertime.

Holding my stomach, willing the cramp to go away, I think about how the new vats couldn't be built fast enough.

———

As the elevator doors open, I see Wiggs waddling toward me. His enormous stomach is spilling over the waistband of his pants. His arms are swinging out from his sides, almost horizontal to the floor. Wiggs's hair is its usual snarled mess, and his long goatee seems even more tangled than normal. He's still about three yards away, but I already catch a whiff of the garlic stench that surrounds him like his own personal atmosphere.

"Hi Sean!" he says, spotting me as I exit the lift. The excitement in his expression tells me he's heard the news.

"Hi," I say, grinning as he approaches.

"Guess what?" Wiggs says, his eyes wide and shining. "With the problems they've been having with the rations, the captain is considering using my vegetables for meals." Wiggs wheezes as he walks. "If that happens, we're going to have to expand hydroponics. Kartak is pretty sure he can rig something for us."

"Yeah, I heard about that," I reply, a little irked. It sounds as if the captain is taking credit for the idea. That's not fair to Waph. I'll have to make sure people know who the idea really came from. Then a thought crosses my mind. "Where will we put the new vats?"

"Your guess is as good as mine," Wiggs replies, coming to a stop beside me. The reek of garlic is even worse up close, sharp and overpowering. It makes my eyes water. "We'll probably have to scrounge any open space we can find in the library, gym, and maybe some of the holds. It will take a lot of space to grow enough food for the whole crew."

"Do you really think we'll be able to expand hydroponics that much?" I ask. "Will we have enough water?"

"I don't know," Wiggs says; he pauses for a moment to catch his breath. "Come on, let's get to the bridge. The captain wants to talk to everyone."

Squeezing around Wiggs's massive frame, I trot ahead of him to the bridge. The hatch slides open. The bridge is filled with excited chatter. Captain Sharta, First Officer Johnson, Engineer Marcum, and all the scientists are here (except for Wiggs, of course; he lumbers through the hatch after me).

"Right, listen up," the captain shouts over the buzz of conversation. His thick mustache leaps up and down as he speaks. His eyes rove around the bridge as if ready to attack anyone who talks out of turn. The noise dies down almost immediately. "I think you've all heard the news, but I'll explain it briefly just to be sure," he says, puffing his chest out importantly as he speaks. "Kartak thinks he has a way to improvise some hydroponics vats. I want Marcum, Wiggs, and Waph to work with him. Any undedicated space will be made available for this. And I've already asked Wiggs to become the ship's cook."

"Great, so now we'll all end up smelling like a field of garlic," Sharden growls.

"Would you rather go hungry?" Wiggs asks, sounding miffed.

Sharden doesn't reply. He obviously can't think of a suitable retort, which is unusual for him.

"That's all," the captain says. "I want you to start gathering the materials right away."

I see Kartak nod. His eyes scan the bridge, and stop when they land on me. "Sean?" he says uncertainly.

"Yes, I'm here."

"Listen," Kartak says. "My eyes are getting better at seeing things in this rainbow light, but I still can't make out details. Would you be willing to help with the project?"

"Definitely," I say, a feeling of importance swelling inside. The new vats will help us survive, and I get to help make them! I can't wait to start.

Kartak smiles. "Great. We'll round up the supplies, and then I'll come and get you."

"I'll be in the lounge," I reply. "Just let me know when."

"You can count on it," he says, and shuffles out the door.

I stand and watch him until my stomach calls attention to itself with a loud rumble. "It is thirty-seven past two," the computer says, before I even ask. Am I becoming that predictable? Now that is just scary.

CHAPTER 2

Deja Vu

"Sean, are you here?" Kartak asks, peering around the lounge.

"Yep, over here." I wave my hand to catch his eye.

Kartak nods in my direction. "Good. We're ready to start," he says, massaging the crooked fingers of his right hand.

"Great!" I say, popping up at once. I take one last look at the tiny ribbons of rainbow outside the viewport – noting that one of them seems to be a bit broader than the others – before following Kartak out the hatch. As we head for the gym – the designated space for the first expansion – I think about how nice it will be to work with Kartak and Waph instead of Roberts. I won't have to respond to the name Rita, or answer questions about what space travel was like in the past. Hopefully, Kartak will tell us stories about the jobs he's had. So far, I've learned that he has worked as a deep core miner; a sonic relay station engineer; the lead hunter on a colony planet; an interstellar cargo runner; the maintenance man in a deep-sea habitation unit; the head technician at a factory that makes Stratagem devices and, most amazing of all, he spent his early teen years as a bull rider. I never tire of listening to the stories he tells. I definitely prefer them to the yarns that Hollins spins – ludicrous adventures that could never happen in real life.

We enter the gym. A pile of materials has been stashed on the right side, filling almost half the room. With the gym equipment shoved against the left-hand wall, that leaves a very small work space in the center of the gym.

"Hey, it's my work partners!" Waph says, glancing up from the mound of equipment.

"There should be a tool box around here somewhere," Kartak mutters. I spot it instantly and hand it to him. "Good. Let's get started."

We work for hours, bending thin pipes, straightening fat pipes, attaching a spaghetti of pipes to large tubs, and basically doing everything imaginable with pipes. Even when Sharden peeks in and mutters a surly "supper", we continue working until, grunting and groaning, we finally manage to force a stubborn pipe into its proper place. Waph and I are left standing here, trying with all our might to hold it steady – my hands shaking with the effort – while Kartak hurriedly fuses it to a valve leading to the vat.

Giving a grunt of satisfaction, he says, "That should do. You can let go. Good job, guys. Now let's go get some chow."

I pat my growling stomach. It can certainly use some food. Unfortunately, all it's going to get is ship's rations that are starting to rot.

I return all the tools to the tool box, seal it up, and set it on a nearby crate. "Lead on," I say, gesturing with my right hand. As I follow Kartak to the hatch, I think with satisfaction about the good news we will be able to announce at dinner. We have a good start on three new hydroponics vats.

Abruptly, something seems to yank me off my feet and I'm flying toward the gym ceiling. Disoriented and panicked, I flap my arms around, trying to gain some control. It's not helping. I'm going to smash into the ceiling soon. There's no avoiding it. I close my eyes, wondering how badly it's going to hurt.

My shoulders smack the ceiling, I rebound, and drift toward a wall. That wasn't so bad. But what's happening? Have we been hit by another asteroid? What if there's a hull breach? My insides seem to freeze at the thought.

"The gravity generator must be down!" Waph exclaims, bumping into me as he glides past.

I groan at the thought. My stomach doesn't like zero-g. On the shuttle up from earth, I filled two bags with barf. I don't want to get sick now; I don't get enough to eat as it is.

As I think about this, I realize that my stomach isn't rebelling. Perhaps it's adjusting to life without gravity.

I reach a wall and push off at an angle toward the floor. I coast downward for a moment, but I never reach the deck; something pushes me away. This is puzzling. When I reach another wall, I decide to launch downward again. The same thing happens: I start angling for the floor, but immediately something pushes against me, preventing me from getting closer than a yard or so from the deck. This isn't zero-g. Gravity has reversed itself again!

A surge of joy rushes through me. We've done it! We've gotten back… but even before I finish this thought, my excitement evaporates. Although gravity seems to have reversed itself again, we haven't returned to normal space. I know, because I'm still surrounded by a rainbow of colors.

———

There is bedlam in the hallway. I grab the hatch frame and stick my head into the corridor. Several scientists are trying to reach the bridge. Marcum, the *Aurora's* engineer, is heading in the opposite direction, trying to get to engineering. None of them are very coordinated in the reverse-gravity. They keep getting in each other's way.

"Let me by!" Marcum demands. "I have to get to the shield generator!"

"I'm trying!" a voice says. Another scientist just grunts.

"It looks like supper's been postponed," I say with a groan. I don't know how much longer I can survive without food.

Kartak glides up beside me, clinging to the hatch frame. "We'll just have to wait until the corridor clears, and then slip into the mess hall for a quick bite."

"What's all the ruckus about?" Waph asks, from somewhere inside the gym.

"Traffic jam," I reply, watching the bodies flail awkwardly like overturned turtles.

Marcum finally makes it through. Roberts, Sharden, Hollins, and my dad all struggle to head forward, pushing off of anything within reach (including each other). They look like a weird, multi-legged creature that's trying to learn to ice skate… and failing spectacularly. I quickly put a hand over my mouth to stifle a giggle.

It takes several minutes, and a lot of grunting and complaining, for them to make it past the gym. I feel a moment of pity for my dad; stuck in the middle of the group, he seems to be getting kicked the most by men trying to propel themselves forward. No doubt tomorrow he'll have bruises everywhere.

Just as I'm about to launch for the mess hall, the computer says, "Sean, Marcum wants you in engineering."

"Of all the lousy –" I keep the rest of the thought to myself. I know it's important that I help Marcum – he'll be working on reversing the shields and gravity again – but I have to eat. I can't go on much longer without food.

"I'll be there in a few minutes," I promise.

"He said to come straight away," says the computer.

"I just have to grab something to eat," I reply, and kick off the hatch frame.

It's quickly apparent that something is different from the first time gravity was reversed. Back then, everything pushed against me: deck, walls, and ceiling. Now it's only the deck that's pushing me away. It takes a few moments for me to adapt to this new twist, but I'm soon gliding easily down the corridor. From the thuds and mutterings coming from behind me, it's clear that Waph and Kartak aren't adjusting nearly so well.

A quick glide through the mess hall, and I reach the galley. One of the cupboards has burst open. Ration packets are scattered around the room, hovering a yard off the floor like a swarm of miniature hoppers. I grab the closest one and tear it open, too hungry to care what it is.

Dark rations crumble into my hand. I lick some up and almost spit them back out. They taste like aspirin dipped in powdered soy sauce, and they're so dry it's hard to swallow. A few bites later, the saltiness overwhelms me. I'm craving a drink. I grab for the cold-water tap, realize the faucet won't work properly in this gravity, and picture the captain's furious glare if he finds out I've wasted even a drop. My thirst seems to double; I'm tempted to risk the captain's anger and try the faucet. After all, where else would I be able to get a drink?

The picture of a large, round man with a wild goatee forms in my mind. Wiggs! The big guy has dishes designed for zero-g. He would have a cup I can use!

The computer has other ideas. "Marcum is waiting," it reminds me as I munch. I lick the last few crumbs from the packet, decide another quick side trip won't hurt, and head for Wiggs's cabin.

"Sean, you know that doesn't lead to engineering," the computer states, as I open a hatch on the left side of the corridor. Giving a small kick behind me, I glide through sickbay.

"I know. I have to see Wiggs first," I say. My voice is rough and gravelly. It's hard to talk when my throat is so dry.

"The captain won't be happy –"

"The captain won't know unless you tell him," I cut in. "You're lucky you don't get thirsty. I need a drink."

I'm almost certain I hear the computer sigh. "Very well. Make it quick," it says.

I exit sickbay into the starboard corridor. Bouncing from wall to wall, I head toward the bow, hoping Wiggs is in his room. I've never been so thirsty in my life!

"Come on in," I hear his voice call through the hatch when I knock. The door slides open and a wall of dense, putrid air hits my face. It smells like someone has used several cloves of garlic to cover the stench of an animal that's been rotting for a week. For a moment I feel some of my supper creeping back up. With a great effort, I fight down the bile and launch into the room.

"If it isn't Sean," Wiggs says, huffing and puffing over by the sink. "What can I do for you?"

"Could I borrow one of your null-g cups? The rations have made me really thirsty."

"Of course! Come on over. Do you want some tea?" he asks, pulling himself slowly along the counter. He opens a cupboard and pulls out a weird-looking cup.

"I can't stay long," I say, grabbing hold of the fridge to stop my glide. "I have to help Marcum with the shields."

"I understand. Here. I'll get you a drop of water." I watch as Wiggs seals the cup against the faucet and fills it part way. "Take it with you," he says, handing me the cup. "You can return it later."

"Thanks!" I say, before taking a long refreshing drink. That feels much better!

"You bet!" Wiggs replies. As I coast to the hatch, he adds, "It's too bad you have to work with Marcum, and not Roberts."

"Too bad for you, maybe, since you won't get to hear Roberts call me Rita. I can't be happier." I hear him chuckle as the hatch slides shut behind me. He might find it funny, but I'm certainly glad working with Roberts is a thing of the past.

"You're late," Marcum growls when I reach engineering.

"I stopped to catch a bite of supper," I explain defensively. "It only took a few min –"

"Every second counts! We're vulnerable until we can get the shields up."

The words are like a slap to the face. I can't help it if I'm starving. Perhaps I was wrong. Working with Marcum might not be better than working with Roberts, if he's in such a foul mood.

"I just –"

"Do you want to get hit by another asteroid?" he storms.

"No," I say, leaning away from him, a bit frightened by his outburst.

"Then let's get started! The captain has brought us to a stop, and we won't budge until the shields get fixed."

This is going to be fun, I think drearily as I start working the bolts on the access panel.

CHAPTER 3

The Wide Ribbon

Work on the vats stops as shields and gravity take priority (and the construction project would be too difficult in this gravity anyway). I'm back to using my spacesuit as a toilet. This doesn't thrill me at all. The peculiar feeling of having a vacuum sucking at me still sends shivers up my spine.

I haven't slept for almost two full days. Marcum insists we keep working until the shields are actually shielding us; he only allows me short snack and bathroom breaks. It's getting hard to keep my eyes open.

"Ouch! Sean, watch what you're doing!" Marcum shouts. With my mind drifting for about the tenth time this hour, I've accidentally poked him in the shoulder with a pair of pointed pliers.

"Sorry!" I say, and try to refocus my mind on the task. "You've pulled it halfway down," I say, gazing at a lever he's working on. "About four more inches should do it."

"You need to be more precise than that!" Marcum snarls. The lack of sleep hasn't improved his mood any. "I don't know how you and Roberts ever managed to get the shields right the first time."

"Half an inch more," I growl back, trying hard to hold on to my temper. I'm doing the best I can. It's his own fault for not letting me sleep!

A tulip person floats in front of me, changing color from yellow to orange. I hear it whisper something, but can't catch the words. It sheds another petal, drifting downward. It's going to sit on my head…

"Sean!" Marcum snaps. My eyes pop open. I glance around to get my bearings. The short doze didn't help. I feel as groggy as ever. "Help me get this turned," he says, indicating a squat cylinder. I return the pliers to their place and get a grip on the cylinder. "Now!" Marcum grunts. I twist with all my strength. There is a pop, and the cylinder settles into its new setting.

"How much longer is it going to be?" a voice inquires from the hatchway. I glance over my shoulder and see the captain hovering there, grasping the frame. His mustache twitches up and down; he's definitely agitated.

"An hour or so," Marcum replies, "unless the boy keeps fumbling the tools and taking naps. Then we might not ever get done."

"Yates, you must stay alert," the captain barks. "We're all counting on you. Don't mess it up!"

"I'm doing my best!" I shout, as anger explodes inside me. I want to kick him in the shin, or pull his mustache out... What am I thinking? I'm definitely too tired to think straight!

"Don't take that attitude with me, boy," the captain rumbles.

"Sorry, sir," I say right away. "I'm just really tired and hungry."

"We all are, boy. We just have to deal with it! Make sure it's an hour or less." Without waiting for a response, the captain turns and heads back up the corridor.

An hour passes. A second one creeps along. I have a headache, and my eyes are burning. The colors of the rainbow blur and split in two, one set slightly to the left of the other.

There is a loud grinding noise and a clunk. "That's got it," Marcum says with a satisfied grunt. "I'll tell the captain. Go get some rest. We'll start on the gravity at 0800 tomorrow."

Rest. That has to be the sweetest word I've ever heard. I zip out the hatch before he can change his mind.

Reaching out to push off the left-hand wall, I misjudge the distance. My hand slips and my head bangs against the wall. The rainbow becomes even blurrier and seems to swirl like a kaleidoscope. It feels as if someone is using a sonic drill on my brain. I wince at the pain.

By the time I can see clearly again, I realize that I've coasted right past my cabin. A little twist in mid-air to redirect my body, a snag of a hatch frame to halt my momentum, and I'm able to reverse direction. Bouncing awkwardly off the far wall, I stray off target and almost smack into the wall right next to my cabin hatch. A quick push with my hands at the last second allows me to successfully guide my body through the hatch, with only a scraped shoulder to show for my near-blunder.

The reverse gravity prevents me from lying down on my bunk. I don't mind one bit. It's more comfortable to sleep hovering in the air, anyway. I curl up, close my eyes, and let the soothing darkness guide me into the world of dreams.

____

"Sean." The voice floats to me down a long tunnel. I can't see who's speaking. "Sean." I don't want to leave. This is where I need to be right now. I ignore the call. "Sean!" The voice is getting more demanding. My eyelids flutter open; something flat and hard is sitting only a couple of inches in front of my face. I push it away reflexively, and realize it's my desk.

"I see you've finally woken up," the computer says.

"Why did you have to wake me?" I ask grouchily.

"You are always complaining about how hungry you are," replies the computer. "It is 0745. If you want to eat before meeting Marcum, you had better get going."

That gets me roused. I still feel like I could sleep for another week, but at least my head no longer feels split open and some of my grogginess is gone.

It takes me less than five minutes to grab and consume a ration bar. My borrowed cup is stashed in a cupboard. After taking a couple of sips, I slide the cup back to its hiding spot behind a pile of dishes and turn to leave. Halfway through my glide, the mess hall hatch opens before me. I react instantly, giving a strong push toward the floor with both hands. This sends me shooting up toward the ceiling, barely quick enough to dodge out of the way as two men come barreling into the room, arms and legs flailing as they spin out of control. Roberts accidentally kicks a chair; it drops toward the floor, but never reaches the deck. Gravity pushes it right back up, directly into Sharden's path. The chair cracks him in the jaw. I have to duck quickly out of the room to hide my snort of laughter.

Filled with glee, I head aft toward engineering.

"Sean, in here," someone whispers from behind me. My heart gives a lurch at the unexpected sound. I flip onto my back as I glide along and look back. I've just passed the hatch to hydroponics. There's no mystery to the whisperer's identity; a garlic breeze seems to be following me down the hallway. "I've got something for you," Wiggs says, still trying to be secretive but having to raise his voice as I drift away. Only his bushy head and shoulders stick into the corridor.

I grab a doorway to halt my momentum. I'm sure it's almost 0800. Marcum will be waiting impatiently. There isn't really time to spare on side trips.

"It will just take a moment," Wiggs promises as if reading my thoughts, stroking his goatee with his free hand.

Something about his earnestness helps me decide. I glance around to make sure Marcum isn't in sight, kick for the outside wall, and rebound through the hatchway to hydroponics, catching a wretched whiff – more than a whiff, actually – of Wiggs's body odor as I pass close to him. I grab hold of a vat and hover. Wiggs launches his great bulk toward me and grabs a handhold on the same vat.

"I discovered these in storage a couple of months back, and I've been growing them for special treats," he says, handing me two pieces of something. They are kind of cone-shaped and the skin feels bumpy. "Go ahead," he says encouragingly. "Taste it."

I put one to my mouth and take a bite. A burst of sweet, juicy flavor spreads over my tongue. Strawberries! I take another bite, finishing the first one. The second strawberry doesn't last much longer. I lick the juice from my fingers.

"Those are delicious," I whisper. "Thanks Wiggs! You're ice!"

"You're welcome, Sean. Just don't go broadcasting this to the others," he whispers back.

Is he kidding? There's no way I'm going to tell anyone about the strawberries. I'm just thrilled that Wiggs has decided to share them with me. They are indeed a treat! "I won't breathe a word of it," I promise secretively.

"Good. Now you'd better scram before Marcum erupts."

"That's for sure. Thanks again!" I say, just before launching for the hatch. I glide quickly to engineering, feeling the happiest I've been since soaring through the rainbow with the tulip people.

The shields are fixed. Gravity is fixed. Work on the new vats resumes. I have no time to relax these days, and I hardly have time to sleep. Between working on the vats, helping Wiggs in hydroponics, and studying, it always feels as if my eyes have barely closed before the computer is prodding me out of bed again.

We wrestle one last pipe into place. Waph solders it. "Ok, done," he says. Both Kartak and I let go of the pipe and flop backward onto the floor. A moment later, I realize that when Waph said "Done", it means we are completely done. The three new vats are ready to go.

"Do you want me to tell the captain they're ready?" I ask, a little of my energy returning at the thought.

"That would be great," Kartak says.

I push myself slowly to my feet. My bones ache, my muscles burn. The new vats are ready, but it will take time to grow anything. We won't be harvesting food from them for several more weeks at least. Still, there is a light at the end of the tunnel.

I plod to the bridge. The hatch opens. I spot the captain hunched over a control panel. He looks busy, so I plop down in a chair to wait.

The ribbons of rainbow outside are mesmerizing and beautiful. I gaze at them, thinking in amazement how each one of them is a star giving off multicolored light.

Something's different, though. I lean forward in the chair, wondering if it's just my imagination. One of the rainbow ribbons is more than twice as broad as the others. We're approaching a sun.

The captain straightens up. He must be done with his task.

"Are we going there, sir?" I ask, eager at the thought of visiting another alien world.

The captain jumps. "What the blazes are you doing, sneaking up like that!" he thunders.

"Sorry, sir. You were busy when I came in, so I waited. I thought you heard the hatch open."

"I still am busy, boy!" he shouts. His fingers twitch with agitation.

I decide to leave the question about the star for another time, when he's in a better mood. News of our completed work should redirect his attention and prevent a hurricane of anger. "I came to tell you that we're finished with the new vats, sir," I say quickly.

"The vats?" he yells, straightening to his full height and taking a step toward me. Something seems to click in his brain. His face relaxes a bit, and his voice returns to normal. "Oh, that's good news. Go tell Wiggs he needs to start on them right away!"

"Yes sir," I say, glancing over his shoulder. It's probably just my imagination, but the ribbon seems even wider than before. How long will it take to get there? Will there be any planets?

Pondering the possibilities, I slip out the hatch and go hunting for Wiggs. He's probably in hydroponics. I turn down the portside corridor. The lounge hatch is open. Someone's talking. I recognize Johnson's voice.

"Even with the new vats, we won't be able to raise enough food for everyone. If the rations spoil completely…" Johnson's voice trails off. I finish his sentence in my head. 'We will all starve.' It's not a pleasant thought. The vats will help with our food shortage, but they won't solve it completely. We have to find a way back to our own space before the rations spoil completely!

CHAPTER 4

The Ring

We are getting close to the star. The solar system has a planet… sort of. When it first appeared in the viewport, it looked like any normal planet – a circular shape set against the multicolored light. Now the *Aurora* is near enough for me to see that the object is ring-shaped.

I think back to some of the classic holo games I've played. Could this object have been created by an alien race? The idea makes my heart speed up. Even from this far out, it's clear that the rim is much, much bigger than the *Aurora*. If aliens constructed it, they would have to have technology far beyond our own.

As we get closer, I decide that the world is natural. It's too large and too rugged to be anything artificial. Would it have centrifugal gravity like the tulip people's planet? With our own gravity now returned to normal, I doubt it. The more I think about it, though, the more I wonder whether gravity on the inside of the rim is different from the gravity on the outward side. And how much gravity would a ring-shaped object have?

"Preliminary data indicates a likely temperature range between negative seven and positive thirty-three degrees," the computer states, responding to an inquiry by the captain.

"What about atmosphere?" the captain rumbles.

"The necessary sensors are still inoperable," the computer replies.

"You were able to give us readings of the other planet," the captain states. His voice is rising in vexation.

"That was because the ship was *in* the atmosphere," the computer replies, its voice as unflustered as always. If the captain was speaking to me that way, I would sure be nervous. "I was able to use different sensors on that occasion."

"We can't take any sensor readings unless we get closer, but I can't risk bringing the *Aurora* near the planet," the captain muses out loud.

"What about using one of the sensor pods?" suggests Kartak.

"Yes!" booms the captain. "Computer, would a pod be able to take readings on the atmosphere?"

"The sensors in a pod should work adequately for the task," the computer replies. "However, the *Aurora* would have to be within two miles of the pod in order to receive transmissions."

"We would have to practically skim the atmosphere," the captain says, almost to himself. "That's not much of an improvement." He stands silent for a moment, obviously thinking the problem through. Puffing out a breath, he says, "We can't do it. It's too risky."

If we can't use a sensor pod, then to me the solution is obvious. I wait for someone else to speak up, but no one says a word. "We could use the lander," I blurt out, no longer able to contain the thought. "It can do a close flyby and gather data. When it gets back, the computer can analyze the data."

"That does make sense," Kartak says. A flush of pride sweeps through me at his affirmation. "I could even get some soil samples –"

"No!" the captain barks, stealing away my brief pat on the back. What could he possibly have against my suggestion? "There will be no landing on the first trip. You must keep a distance of at least seventy thousand feet from the surface."

The spark of pride returns. The captain isn't objecting to my plan, only to the suggestion of taking soil samples. The mission will still be dangerous, but it's a risk we need to take.

"Yates, I want you to go with Kartak," the captain continues. "Be careful out there! We don't know how the planet's gravity works, or whether there are other hazards in this strange space that we don't know about."

"Yes, captain," Kartak responds.

We spill through the bridge door, everyone eager to get to the landing bay. As always, I hang back a bit to avoid ruffling any feathers.

Three elevator trips later, we are all on the lower level. The landing bay is in the forward-most section of the lower deck, below and slightly aft of the bridge. I haven't seen a map, but I imagine the bay doors open almost directly below the environmental machinery just behind the wishbone junction on the upper deck.

This is my first time in the landing bay. The lander looks narrow and sleek, with stubby wings – designed for flight inside an atmosphere. The exhaust nozzles are fairly small and close together, suggesting the engines aren't very powerful. I know it has a cargo bay for equipment and supplies. Estimating how much of the lander is taken up by the cargo bay, I decide that it can probably hold five or six passengers.

How I wish I could be going with them!

I want to explore this new world. There likely won't be much to see from so high up, but it would be great to be close to it. I wonder if Kartak will fly through the middle of the ring? If I was piloting, I would probably spiral around the planet, weaving in and out as if I was painting a candy cane stripe on the surface. That would be the best way to gather as much data as possible.

Kartak and my dad climb aboard the lander. The rest of us stay in the bay as they go through a systems check, even though there isn't anything for us to see.

"Kartak requests permission to lift off in five minutes," the computer states.

"Permission granted," the captain replies. "Clear the bay!" he bellows to us.

I return to the corridor and step to the side. The adults file past me, discussing the upcoming trip. The captain exits last. He glances around to make sure no one is left in the bay and then closes the inner hatch. "Is it sealed?" he asks the computer.

"There is a good seal on the hatch," the computer replies.

The captain doesn't seem to trust the computer completely. He runs two more checks of his own to make sure. I hear a grunt of satisfaction. "Remove air from the bay," he orders.

An alarm blares in the landing bay, muted by the hatch. "Bay will begin to depressurize in three, two, one…" the computer says. A moment later I hear the whirr of giant fans, emptying the bay of air – we can't afford to let any of the precious resource be vented into space.

"Bay doors open," the computer says a short time later. "The lander is exiting."

There is a rush to the elevator. Everyone wants to go up to the bridge to watch the lander's progress. I hurry after them, anxious to know what's happening. We won't be able to watch the lander, of course. It will be too far away to see. But I want to know the moment it returns.

———

"That was amazing," Kartak says as he exits the lander. We all scoot in closer to hear every detail. I'm stuck behind Wiggs and Roberts. I try to peek between them, fail, and scan for a better spot. The only available space is to the captain's left. I hurry over and stand just off of his left shoulder and slightly behind him. I squat down as low as I can get; hopefully I'm out of his view.

"There is an atmosphere, and it appears to be breathable. The sensors detected an abundance of water vapor and microorganisms in the air. With the magnification at maximum, we spotted large areas covered in growths that look similar to Earth trees and bushes, and Yates swore he saw a herd of animals." Kartak's body language betrays his excitement and wonder. My dad nods vigorously at everything Kartak says. It makes me want to hop aboard the lander and speed down to the planet. What kind of animals would live there? What would it be like to smell the trees and feel the dirt beneath my feet? It seems like years since I was standing on firm ground.

"There is obviously some kind of gravity on the planet," my dad adds. "Based on how hard the engines had to work to re-enter orbit, the computer's best estimate is that the gravity is just under one-g."

"I suggest we send a team to the surface," Kartak says. "If there's water in the atmosphere, there's bound to be liquid water on the surface. Increasing our water supply would allow us to build more vats."

I watch the captain's face from over his shoulder. His eyes narrow and his temple twitches as he mulls over the possibility.

"Very well," he says at last. "Kartak, you, Yates, and Sharden will go. Johnson and Hollins, I want you to help them prepare the lander. You will leave at 0900 tomorrow morning."

Sharden gets to be on the first landing party? That's not fair! I'm going to have to wait at least several days… if the captain *ever* lets me go down to the planet.

The day passes slowly. I sit curled up in the lounge, trying to focus on my latest math assignment. The large disc outside the viewport makes it difficult to concentrate. It's so close, and yet I'm not allowed to visit.

I give up on math and go to hydroponics, mainly so I won't have to see the planet out there, tempting me. There really isn't much work to do; I wander around, checking water levels and nutrient solutions, counting strawberries – I can't wait to try more! – and making unnecessary measurements of plant sizes.

Supper time rolls around. I gag down my ration bar. It won't be long before they are totally inedible. Each of us gets a quarter of a tomato and some lettuce for dessert. I long for Mrs. Eldbert's apple pie; our elderly neighbor made the best apple pies in the history of the world. I'm not sure what she did to them to make them so special, but they sure were yummy!

"Wiggs, would you like to play some games?" I ask after supper.

"Sorry Sean, can't," he replies. "I have to take some measurements and run some data for the landing party."

"That's okay, I understand," I mumble, and shuffle out of the room. I wander through the ship, searching for something to do. There isn't anyone in sight. Everyone else has important assignments. I'm not allowed to help with the preparations; not even the smallest task. Why do I have to be so young? If only I was eighteen, maybe they would trust me with *something*, even if it's just to stock the lander with tissues.

Without anything to do, I go to bed early. Thoughts of the mission make it difficult to sleep. What if I sneak aboard the lander? I could be one of the first to explore the new world. That would be so awesome! There would be animals to discover, and I would get to name them. Carrying some kind of weapon would be important; if a carnivore attacked, I would have to quickly figure out its weak spot so I wouldn't become dinner.

What would it be like to walk on a ring-shaped planet? Would animals on the inside of the ring be different from those on the outside (assuming the planet has animals)? And how about plants? Those on the inside of the ring probably wouldn't get much direct sunlight compared to those on the outside. Does the planet have volcanoes? Lakes? It can't really have oceans; there isn't enough space for them.

Before I realize it, it's two in the morning. My mind continues to buzz with thoughts about the planet waiting to be discovered. I try to force myself to relax, but that only makes it worse. Just as I finally feel myself drifting off, the computer jars me back awake.

"Sean, if you want to see them off, you need to get up now."

Feeling slightly dizzy from weariness, I stand up, sway a bit, and lurch off to breakfast. Half a ration package later, I'm stumbling toward the landing bay. Everyone else is already gathered there. Marcum is doing a final inspection of the lander. Johnson is making some last-minute adjustments at the landing bay master control panel. Sharden nods at something the captain has said. He glances my way. I'm quite certain I see a sneer on his face. My fists clench. The senile grouch is mocking me!

The three scientists of the landing party board the lander. "Clear the bay!" the captain shouts, even though he and Johnson are the only two left inside. The bay doors close. There's nothing else to see. I hurry up to the bridge, anxious to follow the lander's progress. The small ship will be too far away to communicate with using the graphic pad; we won't know anything about the mission until they return.

What if they don't return? That's always a possibility. Away missions to a new world are always dangerous, especially here where the laws of physics are so weird. I try not to think about it.

The lander comes into view and rapidly gets smaller. Will this be the last time I ever see them?

———

We gather outside the landing bay. I crane my neck to see the readout. There is less than a minute left on the decontamination process designed to rid the lander's outer hull of any microorganism it may have picked up on the planet. My thoughts flash back to the time at the tulip people's planet when I had to sit in quarantine for almost a full day. Hopefully I will never have to repeat that experience!

The timer reaches zero. I hear a clang as the locking mechanism on the door disengages. The landing bay hatch rumbles upward. After a few more seconds, a hatch on the lander slides open. Kartak and my dad emerge and plod toward us, their shoulders slumped with weariness, yet they both wear pleased smiles. Sharden brings up the rear, a snarl on his face.

"It's like a paradise," Kartak says. "Lush vegetation, warm climate, waterfalls, forests, lakes."

"And animals," my dad adds. "Creatures of all kinds."

"We collected samples of soil, rock, and vegetation," Kartak says. "Plus, we filled the two fifty-gallon tanks with water." The captain gives a low growl at this. Kartak hastily adds, "Don't worry, we ran it through decontamination."

"Right," says the captain, puffing his chest out so far I'm surprised the buttons on his uniform don't go shooting off. "Any trouble with the animals?"

"We saw several different types of predators, but none of them bothered us," replies Kartak.

"Good work. I want the samples offloaded, the water tanks emptied, and the lander ready to go back down in three hours. Wiggs, Waph, and Hollins will go with Kartak this time. Your mission will be to collect data on a different part of the ring, and to collect more water."

"Yes sir," Kartak replies. "Let's get this stuff offloaded right away."

The adults head toward the lander. Nobody invites me to help; even my dad completely ignores me as he hurries by with a sample container in his hands.

I watch them pass to and fro, carrying the samples to a storage compartment for later analysis. The roar of an engine rumbles through the deck from one of the holds. Waph emerges driving a lifter. He maneuvers it into position beside the lander. Johnson and Marcum help wrangle one of the water tubs onto the lifter. Waph reverses, deftly wheels around, and heads to the storage tanks. It's great to hear the splash of water – it is desperately needed – but in no time the two tubs are empty. How much will a hundred gallons of water help?

"This is the last of the samples," my dad calls, as he descends from the lander with a box in his hands.

"Get the lander prepped for the next trip," the captain orders. Catching sight of me, he says, "Clear out, boy. I can't have you getting in the way of the work!"

What? I'm not in anybody's way. I've been staying to the side, well away from where they're working. There isn't any reason to kick me out.

Frustrated, I glare at the captain for a moment, then spin on my heel and leave. Stomping up to the lounge, I throw myself down on a couch and wish I could magically transport myself back to Victoria, or even to the tulip people's planet. Anywhere but here.

———

I haven't been allowed down on the planet. Of course, the captain claims it's too dangerous. How is it any more dangerous for me than for anybody else? I'm quite certain I know more about stealth, hiding, and evading danger than anyone on the ship.

One day runs into another. I've been going out of my mind with boredom. Still, the plants in the new vats are reaching a critical stage, requiring close attention. Time seems to be speeding up again. Which is strange, because the rest of us are moving even slower due to lack of energy. It's getting hard for me to even push myself out of bed in the morning.

Today will be a bit better; Wiggs has invited me over for dinner. I shamble, head down, around the wishbone junction, concentrating on putting one foot in front of the other. When I reach his hatch, I barely have the strength to knock.

"Come in!" Wiggs calls.

The hatch slides open and a burst of song hits my ears. I stop, stupefied. It seems like just a couple of months ago that we celebrated my birthday. Surely it can't be here again already? With such short rations, I'm certain this will be the most dismal birthday dinner ever. I don't really care, as long as it means I get *something* to eat.

Wiggs is over at the stove, dishing up food. Waph, Kartak, and my dad are all sitting on the couch.

"Happy birthday, Sean!" my dad shouts.

"Happy birthday!" the others echo.

"You can sit at my desk," Wiggs adds.

I sit down, glad to be off of my aching legs. "Birthday boy eats first," Wiggs says. As he sets a plate down in front of me, he whispers, "You can have double rations tonight. Just don't tell the captain."

I see the big guy wink as I smile gratefully up at him. I don't really care what it is, I don't care how it tastes, I just want to eat! In fact, I'm so hungry, I don't even wait for the others to get their food. I know it's bad manners, but I dig in right away.

Wiggs has cooked… ravioli? I think that's what it's supposed to be. There are large square shells of pasta filled with something that tastes like spinach. I'm not sure what it is, but I wolf it down all the same.

Once I'm done, I sit and listen to the others eat. Nobody talks. They are too intent on their food. Even though Wiggs has given me double of what I should be getting, it doesn't fill me up. As I listen to the scientists eat, I can still hear my stomach mumbling angrily.

"That was good, Wiggs," my dad says at last, setting his plate down on the floor in front of him.

"Good? That was fantastic!" says Waph, wiping his mouth on his sleeve.

"Thanks," Wiggs says, still chewing his last bit of food.

"Yes, that was delicious," I add, standing up to collect the plates.

"You don't have to do that!" Wiggs protests.

"I know I don't, but I want to," I say, piling the dishes in the sink.

Wiggs hefts himself to his feet and waddles over to the counter beside me. "I was going to bake a cake, but I figured I was already pushing the limit on the food allotment. I was afraid if I used any more, the captain would clap me in chains for mutiny. We'll have to make do with frosting instead."

I laugh at this. I'm not sure I believe his story. The last birthday party Wiggs threw me, he baked a cake. It turned out flat and dense. We ended up eating mainly the frosting. He probably didn't want to risk the embarrassment of another flop.

The frosting is delicious; we eat an entire can of it between us. One glance at my dad makes me howl with laughter. Not only has he done his usual poor job of trimming his goatee – it looks like a toddler took scissors to it while he was sleeping – he now has chocolate frosting smeared across his cheek and clumped in his beard.

"What's so funny?" Kartak asks, watching me laugh.

"Um, well, Dad, you have a bit of frosting on your face. And in your goatee."

"Oh!" he exclaims, jumping up. "I might have to take my shower a day early."

"The captain won't like that," Waph says, wagging a finger at him. "You might find yourself in the brig for gross waste of resources."

"Yeah, the captain will think you and Wiggs are co-conspirators. The two of you can share a cell," Kartak adds, making us all laugh.

"I guess you'll just have to wear it for the night," Wiggs says, chuckling.

"Or eat it," Waph chimes in.

I watch Dad as he tries to scrape the frosting off his face and lick it from his hands. This hasn't been such a bad birthday. I had a decent meal, and now I have entertainment.

Dad rubs his hands on his pants to get the rest of the frosting off. He stops suddenly and digs into a pocket. "I just remembered, I have a present for you," he says, pulling something out.

I'm puzzled by what it could be. There aren't any shops out here in this bizarre place. Did he buy me five presents, one for each year of the mission, before we left?

He places something in my hand. It appears to be a blank piece of paper. I turn it over; there's something on it, but it's hard to make out the image. Then my heart suddenly stops. It's a flat photograph of Mom! Her face is hard to see in this rainbow of light, but her smile is unmistakable. Tears leak from my eyes as I sit here, staring at Mom. I notice that the edges of the photograph are curled and a little tattered; Dad must have had this picture a long time.

I snuffle and swipe my hand across my cheek. "Thanks Dad," I manage to choke out.

"You're welcome, son," he replies, and I hear him sniffle.

A loud trumpeting sound makes me jump. I look up. Wiggs is blowing his nose. Apparently, my dad and I aren't the only ones getting emotional.

"Th," I try to say, but the words don't come out. I clear my throat, and try again. "Thank oo." It still doesn't come out right. I try one last time. "Thank you very much for making this such a special day." I break down crying and run from the cabin, embarrassed to show such weakness in front of the men I respect the most on the *Aurora*. Hurrying to my cabin, I shut myself in, anxious to be alone with Mom.

CHAPTER 5

Stampede!

"The tanks are almost full," the captain announces. "We'll send down one more mission. After that, we'll continue our search for a way home."

"I think Sean should come this time," Kartak says. My ears perk up and my heart rate quickens at these words.

"The boy can't go down!" the captain yells. "It's too dangerous!"

"None of the predators have bothered us," replies Kartak. "It would be good for Sean to stretch his legs a little on the ground. I will look after him."

The captain stands for a long moment, his gaze passing back and forth between Kartak and me. It's obvious what he's going to say. I'm grateful to Kartak for trying, but I can't let myself get excited. I prepare myself for the disappointment…

"Very well," the captain relents, ending with a long puff like a steam engine. Wait. Did I hear that correctly? Is he playing a cruel joke on me? "Yates, you go along to keep an eye on him as well," the captain continues. "And boy, you do exactly what they tell you to do. No fooling around!"

I have to restrain myself from telling him I don't need babysitters. I don't want to risk him changing his mind. "Yes sir," I say meekly, doing my best to hide my eagerness. I'm going to the ring planet! Awesome!

Wiggs walks beside me as we head down to the landing bay. There's a lot I was going to do in hydroponics today. The big guy will have to take my place. I have so much energy, my words come out in a rush. "Don't forget to reset the temperature on the greens. The zambarao might have to be pruned. Also, check the nutrient solution on the beans; I think it might be too rich –"

"Okay, okay, Sean," Wiggs says with a chuckle. "Don't worry. I think I can handle it. You just enjoy your time off." He pauses as we enter the lift. The others have gone on ahead, so we are alone. Even though we're in such an enclosed space, for once I'm not bothered by the odor surrounding Wiggs.

"And keep your eyes open," he continues, as the lift starts descending. "I don't want you to become a snack for a predator, just because you're too focused on fretting about the vats!"

"I won't." Wiggs's eyebrows go up. "I mean, I will keep my eyes open. I won't become a snack," I clarify, laughing.

"Don't forget to grab your suit," Kartak calls as we exit the lift. I'm glad for the reminder; it would really stink to arrive on the surface of the planet, only to find I have to stay inside the lander because I don't have a spacesuit. The trip would be a waste!

I trot to the small rack room across from the lift and grab my suit. Throwing it over my shoulder, I rejoin Wiggs as he huffs and puffs down the corridor.

We enter the landing bay. The lander waits invitingly in the middle of the large room. Glancing at Wiggs, I say, "I'll be back in a couple of hours to check on your work." Leaving him chuckling behind me, I climb the ramp to the lander's hatch.

I find myself in a large cargo space. There are storage compartments along the walls, tie-downs at even intervals along the deck, and the two water tanks at the rear. To my right is a short corridor leading to a narrow door. That must be the flight deck.

I step forward eagerly and wait for the door to slide to the side. I will finally get to see what a cockpit looks like!

My first glimpse into the flight deck reveals a dizzying array of instruments. How does a pilot keep track of it all? It's more cramped than I expected, with a low sloping ceiling. Eight acceleration chairs are crammed into the interior.

"You can sit here," my dad says, indicating a seat to his right. For once I don't argue; it's still not too late for them to kick me off the flight, and I don't want to take any chances! I toss my spacesuit on an empty seat and sit down next to my dad.

"Let me get the safety harness for you." Dad reaches across and goes to work on my crash netting. Again I have to hold in my frustration. He's treating me like a little kid, but I just have to endure it.

I'm sitting directly behind Kartak. I stretch as far as my harness will allow, trying to watch him. His hands dance across various surfaces, manipulating controls. His eyes constantly scan all the readouts. A gentle hum comes from somewhere aft. It quickly builds to a roar and the deck vibrates slightly. A large door slides silently open in front of the lander. My muscles tense up. The ship lifts smoothly, hovers for a moment, and then shoots through the gaping hatchway. We're on our way!

I keep my eyes glued to the cockpit canopy; I don't want to miss anything! At first there isn't anything to see except the vague outline of the planet. Details begin to emerge as we draw nearer: lazy clouds like globs of paint, rugged mountains like the teeth of a cog, sheer cliffs dropping a thousand yards or more straight down, rainbow-colored light sparkling off lakes and rivers, and as we approach the inner surface of the ring, swaying trees. I crane my neck to see as much of the landscape as possible.

Kartak brings us to a smooth landing on a broad grassy field beside a river. A short distance downstream the water cuts through deep walls of rock. He spends a few minutes shutting down systems to standby mode. Turning, he smiles and says, "Welcome to the ring planet. Everyone suit up and let's get outside!"

I don't even wait for him to finish. As soon as I hear the word 'suit' I grab mine and start pulling it on. My hands are almost twitching with excessive energy. It's difficult to control them and get the suit on; the process takes much longer than normal.

Once I'm snug in my suit, I glance over at the others. Roberts is still adjusting his sleeves, sticking his tongue between his crooked teeth as he concentrates. Kartak is already leaving the flight deck. I follow him aft, nervous energy coursing through me. What will it feel like to walk on the surface of a planet again? It won't be smooth like the deck of the *Aurora*. Will I be clumsy? It won't do to trip and fall in front of the adults. I'll have to be extra careful to watch where I step.

Kartak, Roberts, and my dad set to work maneuvering the water tanks onto a small lifter platform. I squeeze past them to see what lies beyond. In the rear of the lander is a small living space: kitchenette, tiny lounge, and cramped bunks stacked against each bulkhead.

"Sean, we're ready," Kartak calls.

"I'm right here," I say, scurrying back to where they're waiting. A large door slides shut behind me, and I realize we're in an airlock. It's pretty cramped with the lift platform and tanks taking up so much space. It would feel uncomfortable in here if I wasn't so excited to see the planet.

The air cycles out (we don't want to waste our precious oxygen by contaminating it with air from the planet; our suits will handle the changes in pressure). The outer door opens; with a great whoosh that nearly knocks me off my feet, fresh clean air from the planet rushes into the airlock. I step out and look around in wonder.

Before me is a strip of rippling grass leading up to the river bank. Grass! It feels like such a long time since I've seen it. The grass gives a bit under my boots; it's a much different feel from the deck of a spaceship.

I look up. It's weird to see the broad strip of planet blocking out the middle of the sky. Living on a ring world would take some getting used to.

To the right, in the mid-distance, there is a forest of bushy trees. I walk around, drinking in the beauty of my surroundings: trees, flowers, small critters flying through the air…

"What is that?" I ask, pointing to the canyon. There is something stretched between the two rocky walls. The others look. Kartak shrugs; he puts the lift platform on hover mode and we move closer to investigate.

I spot more and more of the objects, spanning the top of the canyon like a cluster of bridges. As I get closer, I'm more and more certain that these are structures of some kind. Their design – tube like, with an open tunnel facing downward – reminds me of something. Movement catches my eye; it's some kind of animal, hard to distinguish from the background. More movement reveals several of the creatures on other bridges – if that's what they are.

"I haven't seen anything like it on any of my other trips," Kartak says.

"They look kind of like weaver bird houses," my dad says. I instantly realize he's right. That's what they remind me of. Could they be homes? They are much larger than weaver bird houses; a human could fit comfortably inside one of them.

Hearing a light clang behind me, I whirl around. My head jerks upward in surprise, my blood freezes. There are several shaggy creatures investigating the water tanks. They are huge! In some ways their bodies remind me of polar bears, in some ways they are like sloths, and in some ways there's an almost human quality about them. Perhaps it's their eyes; they seem to be examining and calculating.

I edge toward the lander a few steps, knowing it won't do me any good. There's no way I can get to the airlock quick enough to escape the creatures. Right now their attention is focused on the water tanks, but that might not last.

One of them places a huge forepaw on the lifter. I notice that there are two parts to the paw that spread in opposite directions; it reminds me of the feet of the chameleon Bo keeps as a pet. The two sides of the paw close, gripping the pole that leads to the control panel of the lifter. Another of the creatures lumbers around to the near side of the tanks and starts sniffing. I notice that all four of its feet are split into two halves.

"Be careful," Kartak whispers. "No abrupt movements." His voice is steady, his face calm. Thankfully, a glance at Robert's and Dad's faces reveals that they aren't feeling nearly so unruffled by the situation. I'm glad I'm not the only one whose heart is pounding in terror.

In two swift steps, the nearest creature closes the distance and grabs my wrist. Alarmed, I try to twist away, but its grip is too firm. Even through my suit I can feel that the padding of its paw is surprisingly soft and a bit spongy, so its grasp isn't hurting me. Its other forelimb is swinging toward me… I wince and duck, expecting a powerful swat across my face. Instead, I feel a tapping on my wrist. Because of my suit cuff, I sense only a slight pressure with each flick. Looking up, I see the creature tapping with the back of a claw. It's not a steady beat; sometimes the tapping is faster, sometimes slower.

A series of yelps alerts me to the fact that the adults are receiving the same unusual treatment; Kartak, Roberts, and my dad all have a sloth-bear holding their wrists and tapping. The creatures don't seem to be threatening, so I relax a little.

After a short while my creature pauses and stares intently at me. Once more I get the feeling that the eyes are alert and calculating. When nothing happens, it resumes the tapping, this time against my shoulder, neck, and then forearm. Again it stops and gazes expectantly, as if waiting for… for what? For me to respond? Maybe that's what's happening. Perhaps they are trying to communicate with us! If only the computer was here to test my theory. If this tapping is language, perhaps the computer can decode it the way it figured out the tulip people's language.

I try to pay attention to the rhythm of the tapping, but I can't figure out any pattern. If it is a way of communicating, it's much too complicated for me to pick up.

A sudden loud hooting makes my heart jump. The sloth-bear looks up, drops my arm and lopes quickly away. The other creatures follow. I watch as they pass swiftly into the canyon downriver. Roughly a hundred yards into the canyon, they turn abruptly and swarm up the cliff wall. Before long each of the six creatures is clinging to the underside of a different weaver bird structure. One by one, they disappear inside. Those must be their homes!

"Phew! I'm glad that's over with," my dad mutters, breaking into my thoughts.

"I wonder what spooked them," Roberts says, his voice quavering.

"I don't know," my dad replies, peering anxiously around. "I say we get this done as quickly as possible."

"I agree," Kartak says. "We'll fill the tanks and collect some samples –"

"Do you hear that?" I ask, turning my head to try to locate a muffled roar that's growing steadily louder. My heart pounds painfully in my chest. The sloth-bears are large. If they're scared of something, we should be too. And if something dangerous is making that sound…

Movement catches my eye. I look skyward and see a large flock of birds passing overhead. Several more flocks are approaching from a distance.

With a great crashing of branches, the source of the loud noise comes into view: hundreds of animals of all shapes and sizes break through the line of trees and stampede toward us.

"Into the lander!" Kartak cries, rushing for the lifter controls.

"Leave it!" dad yells, sprinting to the airlock.

I follow quickly on his heels. Kartak continues to wrestle with the water tanks. The thunder of charging animals is deafening, even through my helmet. They will be on us in a few seconds…

Kartak finally seems to accept this, abandons the lifter, and dashes into the airlock. He hits the control just as the first of the animals sweep by. The deck plates tremble with the thunder of their passage.

As soon as the decontamination and airlock cycles are through, we rush to the cockpit. The stampede continues. Even though I don't know any of the local creatures, I'm quite certain the charging mass contains both carnivores and herbivores. The sky is seething with speeding flocks of birds.

"I suggest we raise-ship and head back right away," Roberts says, his face full of awe and anxiety as he gazes out the viewport.

"We have to try to collect the water tanks and lifter," Kartak replies. "The captain would have our hides if we don't. The animals seem to be avoiding the ship, anyway."

"For now," Roberts says. "But they're berserk. It would only take one or two of the bigger ones to damage us."

"I think we'll be okay," Kartak says, settling back in his chair.

I strip off my spacesuit and hang it over the back of a seat. Sitting on the very edge of my chair, I grip the armrests tightly and watch the spectacle outside.

I don't know how long it lasts; it seems like hours. Eventually, the mass of animals thins to a trickle, and finally to a few scattered stragglers.

"I'm going to check the tanks," Kartak announces.

I suit back up and join him. The airlock doors open to an incredible sight.

There is no grass left. It has all been chopped up and trampled into the dirt by the animals. Many smaller trees in the nearby forest have toppled; the larger ones are missing half their branches.

Everything is eerily silent. There isn't even a hint of a breeze; the leaves of the forest droop undisturbed. Something isn't right; I can feel it. A tingle of unease crawls up my spine.

At first there is no sign of the water tanks or lifter. We search all around the lander. Kartak finally spots a weird spiral sticking out of the riverbank upstream. It's the lifter platform! I quickly correct myself. It *was* the lifter platform. It doesn't take a mechanic to realize that the lifter will lift no more. I don't see any way the platform can be straightened out. Also, the control board is gone, with only a tangle of wires to show where it once sat.

A few minutes later, I discover one of the water tanks. It has huge dents in it, so that two opposite sides almost meet in the middle.

"It might still hold some water," Kartak says hopefully. He retrieves the tub, takes it down to the river, and starts to fill it. A fountain of water springs from a hole in the side. Growling in disgust, Kartak hauls the tank back and places it in the airlock.

I notice that it's growing darker. The sun is still high in the sky, so I know night isn't approaching. Then I realize that it also can't be night because on a ring world there isn't much of a proper night; the planet doesn't block the sun enough for it to grow dark for very long. As I'm thinking this through, the reason for the darkness becomes apparent.

Round, lumpy clouds are crowding into the sky, blocking out the light. Unlike clouds on Earth, they all look the same size and shape, as if someone has formed them with a cookie-cutter. I can't help thinking they look like grenades.

Suddenly, thin jagged rainbows flash through the normal rainbow… lightning! It shoots from each cloud in all directions. I see it strike the ground in dozens of spots, sending up little bursts of dirt and plumes of dust. Cracks of thunder peal the sky like explosions. The clouds seem more and more like grenades with every sharp flash and screeching boom.

"Inside!" Kartak yells. The statement is unnecessary. I'm already skidding to a halt next to the crumpled water tank. Kartak hops in after me and hits the portal sensor. The hatch slides across, shutting out the light display, but not completely muting the boom of thunder.

Roberts is waiting outside the airlock door, sucking his teeth, his eyes wide with terror. "I think it's time we were leaving," he says, as soon as we step into the hold.

"I agree," Kartak answers, much to my relief. I don't really want to go back to the *Aurora* quite yet, but I would rather not get stuck in a thunderstorm.

I remove my helmet as I walk toward the flight deck. Straight away I hear a sound like something heavy being dragged across gravel. The noise baffles me. It isn't until I reach the cockpit that I discover what is making the harsh sound: a heavy rain is drumming against the ship. It's almost as dark as night outside. The only light I see is the jagged, rainbow-colored lightning flashing in all directions. I'm sure the lander is built to take lightning strikes, but I'm just as sure that I don't want to take any chances.

Kartak seems to feel the same way. Diving into his seat, he runs his hands across the control board and raises the ship. Immediately, wind buffets the lander, tossing it about like a leaf on a gusty day: up, left, up, left, down. I'm almost thrown off my feet. Grabbing a chair, I slowly pull myself until I'm sitting down. It takes a moment for me to fasten the crash harness.

I hear the sound of retching to my right. It's Roberts. He's vomiting into a bag. I look to my left at my dad. His face is tight. He doesn't look too good. Kartak is staring grimly ahead; his hands dance across the controls as he does everything he can to keep the ship from flipping upside down and spiraling to the ground. The lander shudders and shakes with ominous creaks and groans. Will it hold together? Rain lashes the cockpit window as if desperate to find a way in for shelter.

"We can't make-orbit in these conditions," Kartak says through clenched teeth. "We'll have to try to find shelter."

"What if we go to the other side of the rim?" my dad suggests. "It might not be raining there."

"That's nearly a thousand miles away," Kartak replies without taking his eyes off the viewport. "We'd never make it."

I notice that he keeps the lander low to the ground; if we hit an air pocket, we won't fall far.

Three huge thumps make me jump. A barrage of spheres flashes through the beams of the lander's forward lights, smash against the viewport, and bounce off. Hail! Huge chunks of ice, some almost as big as a cantaloupe, hammer against the lander. I can't look! Every second I expect the viewport to shatter.

Not looking is even worse. Every quake, every drop, every crash of hailstones feels like it will tear the ship apart. I open my eyes and peer out the viewport into the semidarkness. It's hard to see anything, despite the lander's forward lights. I catch brief glimpses of whipping tree branches; large tufts of grass flashing past; and flickering stabs of lightning. Then something catches my eye.

"Over there!" I shout, pointing frantically toward a looming cliff. "I think it's a cave."

"Will it be big enough?" Dad wonders out loud. The sound of vomiting is the only comment Roberts offers.

As we near the yawning black opening, it's clear that the entrance is more than adequate to admit the lander. We slip inside, with several yards to spare on all sides. Instantly, the pounding of hailstones against the lander stops. Whew. I'm glad that's over!

Kartak glides the ship a dozen or so yards farther into the cave. The lander's forward lights form twin rainbow tunnels through blackness. The cave continues onward beyond the light of the lamps; it must delve deeply into the cliff. We should be safe from any weather here.

Once the lander is firmly on the rocky cave floor, Kartak switches the systems to standby. There are no more retching sounds from Roberts, although he still looks queasy and weak.

"Well, what do you say to grabbing a bite to eat and then go exploring for a bit?" Kartak suggests.

This unexpected proposal throws me for a second. After the petrifying flight we just endured, exploring is the last thing on my mind. I was assuming we would sit in the cozy lander and wait out the storm. The thought of heading out into a dark cave on an unknown world doesn't thrill me. But I don't want the others to know I'm nervous. "Sounds like a plan," I say, trying to sound confident and excited. Hopefully they don't hear the quiver in my voice that's evident to me.

"Roberts, we'll get you some fluids," my dad says, unstrapping and helping the weak scientist to his feet.

"I'll go back and get lunch on the table," Kartak says with a smile. He seems to be in his element; the crooked-fingered scientist was born to explore.

Kartak bustles aft. I follow at a slower pace – my legs are feeling quite wobbly… whether from the leftover terror of flying through the hailstorm, or the thought of exploring the cave, I'm not sure. It's probably both.

"Look here," Kartak says in surprise as I enter the kitchenette. "Wiggs slipped us some carrots… and are these strawberries?" The astonishment in his voice grows. "These will be a real treat!"

I help him divide the crumbled rations onto four plates. Kartak chooses two carrots and two strawberries and slices them into halves. He hands me a plate. My strawberry seems bigger than the others. I'm sure Kartak has done this on purpose, and I don't say anything.

I take my plate and sit down at the tiny table (it's not much larger than the cabin desks aboard the *Aurora*). Kartak takes the contents of the fourth plate, dumps them into a mixer, adds some liquid from a plastic pouch, and whips up a smoothie. Ugh. I can't imagine how awful that would taste!

My dad enters, supporting Roberts. They slump down into chairs. Roberts still has a dribble of puke running down his chin. His eyes look wilder than ever. It's hard to remember that he's a smart scientist.

"Here you go," Kartak says, serving the other two men. "Scrumptious meatloaf and a little dessert."

"Thanks," my dad mumbles. "I don't think I've ever had the privilege of eating meatloaf that tastes like salty ashes."

Roberts doesn't touch his drink. He is sitting, hunched over, staring straight ahead. "Drink up," Kartak says heartily. "You need your strength."

Roberts seems to be in a daze, but he obeys, mechanically lifting the glass and taking large slurps. I watch his face expectantly, waiting for the expression of disgust to come, but he shows no reaction to the sludge. The bemused scientist obviously doesn't taste it. He's lucky.

On the other hand, I can taste my meal quite plainly. I wish I couldn't. I shovel my rations in quickly and force them down with great swigs of water (I could care less about sparing water right now). Once the rations are down (at least I think they're down; some of them are trying to sneak back up) I take my time with the carrot and strawberry halves, relishing each bite.

"Right, it looks like everyone's done," Kartak says cheerfully. "Let's suit up and investigate our temporary home."

"I'm not sure it's a good idea for Roberts to go out," my dad says, indicating the woebegone scientist with his head. Roberts has now turned his stare to the bottom of his empty glass, as if thinking it might reveal some great hidden secret.

"He's fine," Kartak replies, waving my father's suggestion aside dismissively. "Aren't you Roberts?"

Roberts sucks in his cheeks, shrugs, and gives a little grunt. Kartak takes it as a sign of agreement. "Let's get going," he says, rubbing his hands together, his excitement evident.

Under the pretense of clearing the dishes, I let the others move ahead. I drag out the routine task, making sure each dish is situated perfectly in the little washer unit. Is there any way I can get out of this exploration party? Some excuse I can use that won't make me look like a complete coward?

My brain freezes up on me. No solution presents itself. I spent over a week trying to convince the captain to let me come down to the surface. Now that I'm here, I want to stay in the ship. How ironic.

Unable to stall any longer, I slowly pull my spacesuit on. My fingers don't work very well. They fumble at the fastenings. Finally, my helmet is in place, my systems check out, and I'm trudging toward the airlock. It's time to leave the safety of the ship, and venture into the black, alien cave.

CHAPTER 6

Neighbors

The rainbow-colored light from our lanterns bobs up and down as we leave the comforting protection of the lander. Kartak has a rifle and an energy pistol. My dad and Roberts both have small hand weapons. I just have the spacesuit and my skin for protection.

Inside my suit, I hear only the muffled whistle of wind and the steady rhythm of my breathing. This won't do. I need to listen for danger, and be able to hear the others when they speak. I turn my external pickups up to full volume. The sounds around me turn louder, crisper: the moan of wind; dripping water; boot steps along the floor of the cave; a dry rasping, barely audible amidst the other noises.

I catch sight of something in the edge of the lamplight, turn my head to the right, and angle the beam of my lamp to bring the objects into view. There is a tangle of branches along the wall. A gust blows through. The branches claw and scrape against the wall, and the dry rasping intensifies momentarily. Mystery solved.

"Branches in a cave. I don't like this," Kartak mutters.

The words sound foreboding, but I don't understand the problem. Why would Kartak care that there are branches in here? It's not like someone's going to come along and turn one into a club or spear. They seem pretty harmless to me.

The cave narrows into a wide passage. Kartak takes the lead. I follow close behind him; I figure if something attacks us, Kartak would have the best chance of fighting it off. I'm not sure if either Roberts or my dad has ever encountered so much as a pet poodle before.

I glance back. Already, the lander is lost in the darkness behind us as if it doesn't even exist. We move from one pocket of blackness to another. The tunnel twists and turns, burrowing deep into the ground. Every step takes us farther from safety. If we get attacked by something now, we won't have much chance of making it back to the lander. I'm not sure my nerves can handle much more of this.

Kartak's lamp flashes on a large opening to the left. A split second later, four beams of light converge at the yawning entrance. "Let's check this out," Kartak says.

I would rather not. We've pushed our luck far enough as it is. Still, I don't want to be left all alone. Instead, I inch closer behind Kartak. He's not getting more than an arm's length away from me.

The cave floor slopes up to the opening. Kartak seems to stiffen when he reaches the threshold. I step to the side to take a peek around him.

The entrance leads to a huge cavern. I can't see the ceiling or the back of it. However, I'm not too interested in those details at the moment anyway; I'm more focused on what's covering the floor.

Everywhere my lamp splashes light, I see animals. Creatures of all sorts – carnivores, herbivores, large, small, sleek, lumpy – are crowded into every pocket of the cavern, many of them lying half on top of their neighbors. My muscles tense up and I turn to run, but realize that none of the animals are moving toward me. In fact, none of them are moving at all. Are they dead?

"Sleeping," Kartak murmurs, seeming to answer my silent question. "Hibernating." Looking closer, I see he's right. The animals are breathing; their chests rise and fall, and small clouds of vapor rise with each breath from the mouths of the largest animals.

"Well I'll be a Q-tip," Roberts exclaims when he steps up beside me. "Would you look at that!" My dad whistles at the sight.

"I think we should be heading back," I suggest, hoping I don't sound as panicked as I feel. What if our lights, or the noise we're making, causes them to wake up? I doubt they would appreciate having their slumber disturbed.

"Sean's right," my dad says, stepping away from the cavern. I'm glad he's backing me up. I'm even happier that his voice sounds as nervous as mine.

"Yeah, I guess so," Kartak says. "Yates, you take the lead. I'll watch the rear."

The trip back seems to take a lot longer than the trip out. I keep expecting a predator to creep up silently from behind and pounce. Even though Kartak is guarding our rear, I constantly crank my head around and shine my light behind us, peering into the darkness to try to spot stealthy shapes.

"What's this?" my dad asks, making my heart jump. I quickly turn from watching our rear to see what he's spotted.

There is another opening, this one a bit smaller than the last one. How did we miss that when we passed it before? Puzzling over the mystery for a moment, I notice that the tunnel turns at this point; perhaps the entrance was hidden as we rounded the bend.

We walk up a short slope to investigate. I know what we'll find before we even reach the opening. A long snout sticking out from the edge of the entrance confirms my suspicions. Soon our lights are shining into another cavern, this one also crammed tight with animals. It's as if all the creatures of the region have decided to throw a giant slumber party.

I see a glint; did that eye blink open? I'm almost certain it did. A creepy feeling snakes up my spine. "Let's get back to the lander!" I say, eager to get away from these animals.

Nobody argues. We return to the main floor of the tunnel. After one turn, the passage expands. We're back in the cave with the lander. After that long, tense walk back I suddenly wish we still had farther to go; that creature-filled cavern is way too close to the ship for comfort.

———

Our second trip into the inner depths of the cave goes much the same as the first. There is a trickle of water that winds through the passage, past our lander, and is lost in the soaked ground outside. We pass by the second cavern full of animals and find a third, fourth, and fifth hibernation center. I never feel safe on the trip, and make sure I stick to Kartak like a shadow.

Our third trip starts routinely enough. We pass the first cavern; a quick peek confirms that the creatures are still sleeping soundly. As we approach the second cavern, I hear muted rumbles. Are some of the animals mumbling in their sleep?

Just as I reach the entrance, I hear a series of snarls and a spine-tingling scream. Our four lamps intersect on the ruckus, and what I see steals the breath from my lungs. A group of mixed carnivores is tearing into one of the largest animals in the cavern. Dozens of eyes turn our way. I hear a chorus of throaty growls and chilling howls. One kind of predator in particular seems to pay close attention to us: it has large, powerful jaws, a sloped back, and a sleek pelt. I count four of them; they all seem to be staring straight at me with pitiless eyes.

"Back to the lander!" Kartak says sternly. I back quickly away, making sure I stay clear of Kartak so I don't trip him as he covers our retreat. I continue to backpedal, my eyes on the stretch of passage we've just traversed, expecting that at any moment I will see a horde of pitiless eyes and powerful, slathering jaws in the bouncing light of our lamps.

We round a bend. There is still no sign of pursuit. Hopefully the predators are content with the kill they've already made. If they've just come out of hibernation, perhaps they still feel a little sluggish.

Then I hear a sound that makes my legs feel weak. There is another chorus of snarls followed by a second agonized scream… only this time the sound comes from *behind* us! The predators in the cavern next to our lander must have awakened as well!

"Easy does it," Kartak says, his voice firm and steady. "Yates, keep your eyes peeled. They're probably too focused on their meal to notice us, but it's best to not take any chances."

His calm, even tone helps me relax a bit. I try to keep an eye on both directions as I stride quickly through the blackness. The cacophony of sounds grows louder. Some of the creatures sound close enough to touch. My eyes work overtime, trying to pierce the rock walls and darkness around me to locate all threats. I catch sight of the cavern entrance. There is a clamor and a thrashing of bodies just inside the opening. I spot several more of the strong-jawed carnivores, along with numerous smaller creatures.

We draw even with the cavern. Two of the largest carnivores halt their gorging and take a step toward us; they look angry that we've disturbed their meal.

"Run!" Kartak commands, bringing the rifle to his shoulder and drawing a bead. I feel torn between putting as much distance as possible between me and the predators, and leaving Kartak all alone to face the beasts. If we leave him and run, will he be able to fend them off if they attack? I don't have a weapon, but it still feels like abandoning Kartak, forcing him to stand alone.

"I said run!" he snaps, his voice urging us on. I jog through the tunnel, my upper body half-twisted around so that I can watch behind me.

I'm amazed at Kartak's skill. He is shining his lamp along the barrel of the rifle. He continues to retreat, gliding smoothly but quickly backward, negotiating the twisting path of the tunnel.

Soon we are in the lander's cave. Roberts is running unsteadily a few feet ahead of me. At first I'm not sure where my dad is. But as Roberts stumbles a bit and lurches to the left, I spot him; he is already crouching down in the cover of the lander. The coward sprinted ahead, leaving Kartak to defend us by himself!

"Okay Kartak, I have you covered," my dad says. "You can sprint home."

Now I see that my dad has indeed turned around, and he's using the lander to steady his energy pistol as he aims back up the tunnel. Perhaps I misjudged him; he wasn't sprinting to save his own hide. He was getting into position to help Kartak.

"Come on, Sean, move it!" Kartak growls. Startled, I realize that he has passed me.

At that moment, I see a flash of light from my dad's hand gun. Behind me I hear a terrible screech, almost like an angry hog. I look over my shoulder. A strong-jaw is running back toward the tunnel. It seems to be favoring its left side.

One of them did follow us! The creature moves beyond the beam of light and vanishes from sight. But where there's one… I sweep my lamp around as I scoot toward the ship, desperate to spot anything that might be lurking out there, skirting the light where we can't see. Nothing. Yet it's foolish to assume that just because I can't see any strong-jaws in the narrow beam of my lamp, there aren't any there.

"Good shot," Kartak grunts, breathing heavily from his sprint.

"If it had been a good shot, that beast would have dropped dead," my dad replies, still covering the back of the cave with his pistol.

I put my head down and sprint the remaining distance to the airlock. My dad backpedals, keeping a wary eye on the back of the cave. Kartak helps him step up to the airlock. The door slides shut, and the decontamination process begins. We are safe!

CHAPTER 7

Hunter or Hunted?

The mood at dinner is somber.

"Our air quality won't be good much longer," Kartak says. The lander isn't big enough for a self-sustaining environmental system. It's designed for short-term use. "We're also running out of food. If the weather doesn't clear in the next 24 hours, we're in trouble."

I munch in silence, wondering if this is one of my last meals. It's not what I would choose for a final dinner: dry, crumbly rations that taste more and more like a bouillon cube with each passing day, and a quarter of a carrot – the last one – that's so old and rubbery, I can bend it all the way back without breaking it.

"This storm isn't going to lift any time soon," Roberts says with a snort. "I get the feeling it's just getting started."

"I'm afraid you're right," Kartak says wistfully. The expression on his face makes him look as if he's eating something nasty (since he hasn't touched his food yet, I know this isn't the cause). After a moment of thoughtful silence, he makes a proposal that shocks me. "We should try the meat of one of the animals."

"What!" I say, forgetting all about the rubbery, half-chewed carrot in my mouth.

"That could make us sick," Roberts protests.

"I know!" Kartak snarls. Now I know why he's wearing that expression. He's the one who tested the tulip people's food. He's the one who got violently sick and almost died as a result. It has to be extremely hard for him to consider trying more alien food. "But it's either that or starve," he points out grimly. What a rotten choice. Would I rather die of starvation, or die of violent illness?

"We don't need to make a decision until tomorrow," my dad points out. "Let's not worry about it until then."

How can I not worry about it? We're going to have to wrestle one of those animals away from the carnivores, butcher it, and see whether it kills us. We'll probably have to eat it raw. I've never had raw meat before; that in itself might be enough to kill us. And my dad thinks I'm not going to worry about it?

When bedtime comes, I crawl into the sleeve on my tiny bunk. It's barely big enough for me. I don't know how the grownups manage to sleep on these beds.

My mind gnaws over tomorrow's problems. We will have to somehow crack open a hatch, so that outside air can circulate through, but menacing predators can't. We'll have to risk breathing the alien atmosphere, exposing our bodies to whatever nasty germs it may have. We are going to have a showdown with the strong-jaws and other carnivores. And we'll be munching on meat that will probably cause us to die in horrible agony. Of course, the typhoon could suddenly blow itself out, allowing us to return to the haven of the *Aurora*. Or a giant asteroid could strike the planet and finish us off in one swift stroke.

I drift off to sleep, hundreds of possibilities jostling around in my mind. Few of them are very comforting.

When I wake up, I find the adults in the kitchenette. Kartak is wearing his spacesuit, minus the helmet. Two of the energy pistols are holstered at his waist. "It's time," he says, pulling on his second glove. "We need to find out what the situation is outside. I'll go see if the predators are still on the prowl."

"I'm coming with you," my dad puts in quickly. He half-rises from his seat, I assume to get his suit. Kartak puts a gloved hand on his shoulder to prevent him from standing.

"It's too dangerous," the crooked-finger scientist counters. "We should only risk one person, and I'm the best man for the job."

"What if something happens to you? Who will fly the lander?" my dad asks. His face shows clearly that he doesn't like the thought of Kartak going out alone.

"I could fly it in a pinch," Roberts chimes in. His wild eyes don't inspire confidence.

I wait for someone to protest. I sure want to; a blind three-year-old probably has more flying skill than Roberts. Instead, Kartak says, "That's settled then."

My dad doesn't look happy, but he nods in agreement. "Okay, but only a quick survey. I expect you back within ten minutes."

Kartak looks like he's about to argue, then shrugs his shoulders and heads for the airlock. "Your helmet," I remind him, glad that I can contribute to his protection in some way.

"I'm not going to take it," Kartak replies calmly. "It would just limit my field of view. I'm only wearing the suit for added warmth."

"Oh," I reply, feeling foolish that I've forgotten about the dwindling air supply.

Kartak nods to us as the airlock door slides shut. I head to the cockpit, anxious to watch his progress through the viewport.

A rainbow-colored beam suddenly cuts through the black stillness. I notice that the trickle of water has become a meandering brook about two feet across. The source of the beam comes into view. What's really weird is that I can't see Kartak. Because our brave scout is behind the lamp, its glow does not illuminate him. The light seems to originate from thin air.

The rainbow beam slowly sweeps from side to side for a minute or two, illuminating rocky walls and bundles of branches, and then progresses slowly toward the rear of the cave. The shaft of light grows shorter as the forward portion is blocked by a curve in the tunnel wall. Soon, the last lingering trail is extinguished.

The tense waiting begins.

It reminds me of the hours I spent alone aboard the *Aurora*, after we were hit by asteroids, waiting for news of the damage and wondering if everyone was safe. I'm not alone right now, but the tension is the same. I don't want anything to happen to Kartak.

I find that I'm biting my nails, but it doesn't bother me. Why worry about such trifles as chewed nails when Kartak is in mortal danger?

Minutes pass. My eyes strain for a glimpse of light, the first little sliver of glow that will herald the return of the powerful beam of the lamp. How long has it been? Five minutes? Ten?

Still there is no sign of Kartak. Is he making a last stand against a gang of alien carnivores? Is he lying dead, surrounded by strong-jaws howling triumphantly?

And then I see it: a flash of light. At first I think it's just a trick of my straining eyes; but it soon returns, and grows longer. The beam turns toward us, and I know that Kartak is now back in the cave. He's not safe yet, but just knowing he's still alive is reassuring. A few long minutes later, the shaft of light disappears from view. I race to the airlock, with Roberts and my dad hard on my heels.

The hatch slides open. Kartak is standing there, with no visible sign of injury. Behind him I note that the outer hatch is open a crack. I can hear wind moaning through the cave.

"Everyone is bedded back down," Kartak says, smiling easily. "We'll have our pick of meat. I was going to bring some small game back for supper, but decided it would be better to get a big one that will last a while. The fewer hunting trips we need to make, the better. I couldn't handle it on my own."

This is the best news I've heard in a while. Hopefully the carnivores will sleep for a nice, long time.

"I'll go get my suit and help you," my dad says, heading back toward the cockpit.

"I'm coming too!" I say, the thrill of the hunt filling my veins.

"No!" my dad says emphatically, turning around. "It's too dangerous."

"Let him come, Yates," Kartak says. "It should be safe enough for now."

My dad stands stewing for a while, staring at me as if I've committed some awful crime. "Fine," he growls at last, holding his glare for a moment longer. "But if one of us says run, you bust your butt back here without looking back, you hear?"

I nod. It doesn't seem like the right time to point out that the strong-jaws might run faster than me, and turning my back on them would give them an easier target. That's a river I'll cross if I have to.

Suited up, the three of us gather at the outer hatch.

"Ready?" Kartak asks, fingering a holstered handgun.

"Yes," I say. My dad just nods.

"Here we go." Kartak slaps the sensor. The outer hatch opens the rest of the way, and we step out into the chill wind.

All around me is the deep scent of wet vegetation and the sweet fragrance of flowers, like hydroponics but different, as if these plants are distant cousins of those aboard the *Aurora*. There must be a lush, untamed tangle of plants somewhere just outside the cave. Barely audible above the whistle of wind is the gurgle of water as it flows past the lander. My ears are already feeling the nip; a woolen hat would be nice right now. I don't say anything, fearing my dad would use any excuse to send me back inside.

We trudge through the cave, Kartak in front, my dad next, me bringing up the rear. Before I know it, we are entering the tunnel. The force of the wind is even stronger in here. I stay as close as possible behind my dad; he provides a bit of a shield from the howling air.

The cavern entrance looms to our left. All is silent within. There is no trace of yesterday's carnage; even the bones – assuming these creatures have bones – have mysteriously disappeared.

"I say we take this boy here," Kartak whispers, pointing to an animal the size of a sun bear, that looks like a mad scientist has experimented with breeding an aardvark, a beaver, and an ant. It doesn't look very appetizing to me. I also don't like the fact that Kartak and my dad will have to climb over several other creatures in order to reach it. How soundly are they sleeping? Will a little nudge jar them awake?

The two scientists make it to the targeted prey without creating an uproar. Now comes the next question: what will it take to slaughter the creature? Where is its weak spot? How much noise will it make? How much will it thrash? How long will it take to die? I'm beginning to realize just how tricky the situation is… and how many things can quickly go wrong.

My muscles tense as I watch my dad straddle the creature and grip its head with both his knees and his hands. Kartak makes a quick slice. Lifting its head with a jerk that bucks my dad off – he sprawls onto the side of a slumbering giant – the creature gives a short bellow, which quickly turns to a gurgle, and finally a rasping gasp. Its head slumps back to the floor of the cave. Its legs twitch for a few seconds, and then it becomes completely still.

Kartak immediately goes to work carving it up. He uses the chest of a nearby beast as a table, piling it high with large slabs of meat. It becomes apparent that there is no way we will be able to carry it all back with us.

"It'll take two trips," Kartak says, straightening up and stretching out his back. "Sean, come and help us."

Gulping with apprehension, I step carefully over the head of one sleeping creature, crawl as lightly as possible over the belly of a large beast, and slide to the floor where the remains of our prey lies. Kartak hands me a couple of chunks. Goosebumps crawl up my skin. The meat feels squishy, gushy, and oozes a thick liquid which trickles down my gloves and drips to the floor. Will I really have to eat this? My stomach churns at the thought.

Making my way carefully back to the cavern entrance, I wait for Kartak and my dad to collect their loads and join me. A nearby slumbering giant stirs and moans, making my heart thump. I prepare myself to flee… but a second later the enormous beast resumes its peaceful snooze. Perhaps the scent of the nearby kill somehow penetrated its serene doze.

The trip back to the lander goes without a hitch. We pile the meat into a large metal tub and head back. The second trip goes just as smoothly. As soon as I've dropped my dripping load into the container, I take my gloves to the brook and give them a good scrub.

———

"That should be good enough," Kartak says, as I carry one last bundle of twigs and lay it along one side of our small pyramid of brush. "Stand back," the middle-aged scientist orders.

After making sure we are standing well back, he flicks a switch on his igniter, and touches the small hot flame to the kindling. Once the wood catches, Kartak extinguishes the igniter and returns the disc-shaped device to a pocket of his spacesuit.

The fire looks unusual; there aren't any dancing, flickering flames. It's more of a swirling rainbow glow. The warmth heats my face despite the fact that I'm almost three yards away.

"This sure does burn hot," Kartak comments, as he takes two hasty steps back.

"Let's get the meat on it," Dad says, holding up several dripping bundles.

"You probably don't have to put them directly into the fire," Kartak says. "The rocks nearby will likely be hot enough to cook them."

Leaning back from the flames to protect his face, my dad sidles toward the fire. He stops about a yard away. It's obvious the fire is too hot for him to approach any closer. He tosses the slabs of meat toward the blaze and quickly backs away.

"The flames are dying down," Roberts says. This is an understatement. The fire is already half the size it was when it started, and it's shrinking with every passing second.

"Those branches burn really fast," Kartak comments. "We're going to need more."

I quickly gather a handful of brush. The heat isn't as intense now. I'm able to get within a couple of steps of the flames. I toss my load onto the fire and leap back as sparks shoot up and flames billow out, looking more like colorful smoke than tongues of fire.

I suddenly freeze as an awful wailing, screeching fills the cave. It sounds as if enraged boars are squealing and cats are yowling and rusty hinges are screeching and banshees are shrieking, but a hundred times worse.

"Quick, grab some of the meat!" Kartak yells. My dad dashes to the fire and picks up a chunk. He reaches for another, but Kartak shouts, "Leave the rest! Hopefully we can get it later." He is directing his lantern toward the rear of the cave. A wild mass of bodies rounds the bend and comes charging toward us, yowling and snarling. Strong-jaws!

I turn toward the lander, stumble, fall to my hands and knees, scramble back to my feet, and sprint toward the airlock door. A bone-chilling opera of hissing and snapping plays behind me. It sounds like the strong-jaws are within pouncing distance. I can't spare a moment to look back.

"Come on, Sean!" my dad calls anxiously, waving me forward. Kartak slides to a stop on his knees, spins, and draws a bead over my shoulder. I run, expecting at any second to feel sharp claws ripping into my skin.

There is a moment of confusion as I slam into the back wall of the airlock, Kartak discharges several shots, my dad shouts for him to get in, and powerful bodies try to force their way past the closing hatch. The door jams as a strong-jaw's head prevents it from closing all the way. Other predators stretch their paws through the gap, slashing the air bare inches from where we're plastered against the far wall. The inner hatch opens, but we can't risk trying to slip through; there's too great a chance of getting sliced open by the cruel claws.

Kartak, cool and level-headed as always, aims a pistol from his hip and fires at a flailing leg. One beast retreats, and then a second, third, and fourth. Finally, our way is clear. We tumble into the cargo hold of the lander, Kartak hits the sensor, and the inner hatch slams shut on our nightmare.

I'm on my hands and knees, my muscles rigid, my heart racing. The strong-jaws' shrieks are not as loud in here, but they still send tingles up my spine. I can't get the image of their cold stares, frightening claws, and slobbering jaws from my mind.

"It's a little on the rare side, but it's better than eating it raw," Kartak comments blithely as he accepts the meat from my dad. "Give me a moment and dinner will be served."

I stare at him, wondering how he can be so lighthearted after that near-catastrophe. The crooked-fingered scientist bounces into the kitchenette, humming a lively tune. My heart is still hammering, and my legs are too weak to raise me to my feet. I collapse to the deck, wondering if Kartak would object to delivering room service to me right here. I suppose if worse comes to worst, I could crawl to the kitchenette. Maybe.

"Come and get it! Dinner's on the table," Kartak calls through the open hatchway.

Okay, it's time to try moving. I get my arms under me, and a moment later I surprisingly find myself on my feet. My steps are unsteady, but they do the job. I sink into a chair, wondering how long my heart can keep up this pounding. Surely it can't be good for my health.

I look at the meat on my plate. Is it safe to eat? Or will the alien protein go to war against my body? The tulip people's food almost killed Kartak. I see no reason why this will be any different.

With the image of Kartak, pale and vomiting, clearly in my mind, I hesitantly place a slice in my mouth and take a bite.

The meat tastes kind of sweet, yet gamey; it's the weird sort of flavor Wiggs might produce in his rainbow-lit kitchen… minus the garlic flavor, of course. Speaking of garlic, a couple of cloves with some salt and pepper would be awfully good right now. Or maybe a thick, zesty barbeque sauce with Mom's homemade pecan pie for dessert. The thought makes my mouth water.

I chew, swallow, and wait. My stomach doesn't seem to be protesting. Encouraged, I take a second bite, and wait. Still no sign of my tummy preparing for war. After this I dig in greedily, quickly finishing the rest of the plate.

I sit back with a sigh, feeling full for the first time in months. These alien steaks aren't so bad. The thought reminds me of the carnivores, and I realize I no longer hear their awful chorus. Hopefully they've slunk back to their hibernation chamber. This nice dinner also seems to have calmed my heart. It's back to its normal cruising speed.

"Who's up for some *karata*?" Kartak asks.

I moan. Normally I love games, but we've played cards every single day since landing on the planet, and I haven't won a single game. "Count me out. I'll just watch."

"Come on, Sean. That's no fun," Kartak says.

Losing all the time isn't any fun, either. He doesn't seem to understand this. Seeing Kartak's eager face, I cave in. "Okay, I'll play." After all, my luck has to change some time.

After cards, I snuggle up in my bunk. My thoughts meander from my friends back home, to the tulip people, to Mom, to the *Aurora* (I wonder if they're getting worried about us?), and finally, I think about the creatures we met on our first day here, the ones that seem to communicate by tapping. Their homes, the ones that look like weaver bird houses, must be miserable in this monsoon. I find myself feeling sorry for the sloth-bears, but then I remember that the entrances to their homes face downward; they should be protected from the weather. The only risk would be if a wall of water came thundering down the canyon. Even so, I imagine their homes get shaken quite roughly by the wind. It wouldn't be fun in there.

Did they know the storm was coming? They must have. That's why they left so abruptly. Perhaps they were using the taps to try to warn us about the storm! Or could they have been inviting us to shelter with them? I'm starting to get carried away here! The taps probably weren't language at all. Perhaps the sloth-bears aren't intelligent; simply curious, the way a dog or monkey might be.

And of course, they didn't see *us*: our skin, our hair; they merely saw our spacesuits. With the tint of our helmets, they may not have even seen our faces, depending on how dark our faceplates were at the time, and the angle they were looking from. Even if they are intelligent, it's doubtful they could tell that we're living beings.

"Ow!" I moan out loud, as my stomach cramps momentarily. The pain leaves me breathless. Again my stomach cramps. It gets worse every second. My stomach is going to war after all. I curl up in a tight ball and have to fight to keep from crying out in agony.

Is this it? Am I going to die?

"Are you okay?" a voice asks. The only answer I can give is a moan.

"Is there something we can give him?" another voice asks.

"I'll go check the medkit."

Many agonizing moments later, a hand gently shakes my shoulder. "Suck on this. It might help," a voice whispers in my ear.

I can barely open my mouth. I feel something small and powdery slipped between my lips by crooked fingers. A tart sensation spreads across my tongue and trickles down my throat. It doesn't seem to work. My stomach still feels as if a giant wasp is inside, trying to set the record for the world's longest wasp sting. It hurts so much!

After a long time, the pain eases up a bit. Slowly, very slowly, the agony fades away, until only a slight ache remains.

After carefully composing my face, I turn over and see that all three adults are hovering over me. They don't seem to be in any pain. Why is this happening to me? Am I weak?

"How do you feel?" Kartak asks, watching me anxiously.

"Not good," I admit weakly. "But a bit better. Thanks."

"You must have eaten too much," Kartak says. "I was foolish for giving you so much."

"Do you really think that's all it is?" my dad asks, sounding doubtful.

"The meat didn't affect us," Kartak replies. "And the pill seems to be working. Remember, we've all been on low rations for several months. It's not good to suddenly eat a large meal. We'll have to be more careful in the future."

The last traces of pain ooze away, leaving me feeling exhausted. "My stomach's okay now. I'm ready for some sleep," I say

Kartak nods. "Just let us know if you need anything."

My dad stares at me, looking doubtful. I don't want him to start thinking he needs to baby me. Trying to look relaxed and sleepy, I say, "Don't worry, Dad. I'm fine."

He continues to stare at me until Kartak puts a hand on his shoulder. "He needs rest."

My dad glances at him and gives a short nod. Still looking unsure, he allows Kartak to lead him away. Roberts remains at my bunk for a moment, his cheeks sucked in, his crooked teeth peeking between his lips. I turn onto my other side, so that I'm facing the wall. Roberts sucks at his teeth for a short while longer, and then I hear him plod off to his bunk.

Is Kartak right? Did I eat too much, or can my stomach not handle the meat? Do I really want to risk eating it again? I don't want another stomachache like tonight's. I hope the storm is over soon!

CHAPTER 8

The Stream

Every day, the lander seems to shrink. I thought the *Aurora* felt cramped. Compared to the lander, the *Aurora* is practically a country. And there's nothing to do here – I would even be happy for some school work right now!

I've counted five weather cycles since we abandoned our spacesuits: explosive lightning; ice-chill, gale-force winds; torrential rain; terrifying hail. These repeat over and over again. It's as if each type of weather has its own zone, and the ring planet passes through each one as it revolves.

So far, there hasn't been even the slightest pause in the storm. Unless it sleeps when we sleep and wakes when we do. A storm that follows the sleep patterns of humans? It's a ludicrous idea, but given all the weird things I've seen in this bizarre region of space, even something that far-fetched wouldn't surprise me.

Every meal the meat gives me a slight tummy ache, but nothing like that first night. A little variety in our diet would be nice – eating the same meat is getting tiresome. I'm not complaining, though. Our meals are larger than they were aboard the *Aurora*. We're not on the edge of starvation.

Our food supply is running low again. We'll have to collect more meat in the next day or two.

After carefully sweeping a lamp through the cockpit window to make sure the cave is clear, I head out to see if it's still raining. Two steps from the ship, I hear a scream that sends a shiver up my spine; it sounds almost exactly like the Tasmanian Devil robot I used in my last game of Stratagem, the day Mom died. I retreat hastily inside. Memories flow into my head as the airlock door slides shut: rushing at Hoss; excited at my win; the words that changed my universe.

A deep sadness creeps through me, an old wound that hasn't healed; it may never heal.

Kartak is pulling on his suit. My dad is grabbing his off a chair. "The strong-jaws are active again. We'll have to wait until they settle down before we can collect more food," I inform them.

Kartak winces at the news. "It would be best if we could hunt today. I don't want to risk running out of food. Still, we can't go out if the predators are prowling. Let's check again in a few hours." He starts pulling off his spacesuit. My dad tosses his back onto the chair. We settle down to wait.

With little to do, time trickles by. I could help Roberts – he's tinkering with something in the engine room – but sitting here, staring at the wall is preferable to working with him.

Then I remember my branches. I grabbed them last time I was out in the cave. Roberts grumbled that, "You're cluttering up the space," and "the lander isn't a trash heap," but I ignored him. A huddle of three or four branches in the corner of the hold isn't going to hurt anyone.

I gaze over my options. The longest one is for a bow. It will be crude – utility cord for the string, and I'm not sure what I'll do for feathers on the arrows – but it'll be something to do. However, I'll keep that for later. Right now I have another project in mind.

After selecting a branch and stripping the twigs and leaves from it, I get to work with a small knife. I can feel Kartak's and my dad's curious eyes on me as I whittle. It makes me uncomfortable. I try my best to shield my work from them. If one of them sees it, he would laugh.

"Do you think the *Aurora's* still here?" my dad asks, breaking the silence.

"I can't see the captain abandoning us," Kartak says, and gives a twisted grin. "He knows I'm too tough to die."

"But how would they know about the weather?" I ask, pausing my work to speak the thought that's been on my mind the past few days. "I doubt the sensors would detect it, and I don't think their eyes are sharp enough to see the clouds. They won't know what's keeping us. They might think we've crashed or something." It feels good to get these thoughts out into the open. Hopefully, one of the scientists will be able to point out a flaw in my reasoning.

"They know, Sean, don't you worry about that," Kartak says.

They know? What kind of answer is that? This tells me that Kartak doesn't have a real answer to my question. The captain probably thinks we're dead. The *Aurora* is sure to be long gone. Which means this planet is our home now. It's not a very comforting thought.

"I wonder if they have any new vats set up," I say, to change the subject. I try to force my mind off of thoughts of abandonment, and onto the plants I was tending before coming down to the ring planet. The new vats should be starting to produce any day now.

"There were enough parts for three or four more, but we talked about keeping them for spares," Kartak says. "They may have built one more, if they could handle the job without us." That mischievous grin returns.

I smile back. "They would definitely be lost without us." Bending down, I resume my whittling.

"What are you working on, anyway?" Kartak asks, stepping over to look at my sculpture.

"An eagle," I admit sheepishly.

He grins. "So far it looks more like a gargoyle."

Gazing at the long, lopsided face and crooked beak, I have to agree. And, of course, this gouge I took out of the neck isn't helping the eagle's appearance. "I never claimed to be Michelangelo," I say, feeling color creep up my face. "It's just something to pass the time."

"Keep working at it, you'll get it. But not now. The strong-jaws should have finished their nosing around," Kartak states, patting my shoulder. "Let's go take a peek."

I nod, glad his attention has steered away from my disastrous art piece. Tossing the unfinished gargoyle onto my bunk, I slide my knife back into its sheath and prepare for the mission.

We suit up against the chill, sweep a beam of light through the cockpit window to check for signs of activity, and gather in the airlock. Kartak and my dad flick on the status screens of a rifle and two energy pistols. Kartak grunts and my dad gives a nod; both are satisfied with the power level of their weapons. The crooked-fingered scientist then shines a lamp through the narrow gap between the airlock hatch and bulkhead.

"No sign of fuzzy critters," he announces, slapping the hatch sensor, and swinging his rifle into position as the door slides open. "All seems quiet. Stay near the ship. I'll scout ahead to make sure they're all tucked in."

I watch as he advances through the cave. The gurgling brook is now a frothing stream too wide to jump. Kartak hugs the wall as he reaches the rear of the cave to keep from sloshing through the water. When his lamp beam disappears into the tunnel, I head toward the dim light of the cave entrance to check the weather.

Rain. That's the part of the cycle it's on now: driving spears of water that attack the boggy ground. I gaze toward the sky, hoping to catch a glimpse of an interstellar ship, but my eyes can't make out anything through the haze.

I head back toward the lander, wondering how long it will be until Kartak returns. My dad is keeping a sharp lookout toward the tunnel. His hand rests on an energy pistol.

I'm about halfway back to the ship when a roaring sound reaches my ears. At first it's hard to tell where it's coming from; it seems to be all around me. I turn back toward the cave entrance, thinking perhaps the rain has given way to the howling wind. After a moment, I grow certain that the sound is behind me, back toward the lander. Wondering what it could be, I turn my light toward the noise. I stop in shock. A wall of water is rushing at me through the cave!

My dad starts toward the airlock, seems to realize he won't make it, and hops onto a ledge along the wall of the cave. For me there's no escape.

Bracing myself, I take a deep breath, and then a wave of raging cold water slams brutally into me. Tossed around, I'm completely disorientated; I don't know which way is up and which way is down; all around me is a noise of rushing and roaring; I can't hold my breath much longer!

My shoulder scrapes against rock. I grasp desperately. My fingers find a ledge. Pulling with all my might, I get my head above water. All I can do is cough and sputter and take short, gasping breaths that don't do much good.

Fighting the tug of the current, I slowly inch upward. My head is above the level of the ledge; now my shoulders are. I cough some more and try to take a deeper breath. My muscles tremble with the strain of fighting the torrent. I gather my strength for the next effort. But it never comes. Another surge of water rips my hands from the ledge. The last thing I see is my dad's horror-stricken face bathed in the light of his lamp.

There is complete upheaval. I'm tumbled and jumbled around. My chest is compressing. I can't breathe. Everything is dizziness and roaring and confusion. There's no way to fight it and no way out.

This eventually passes into a nightmare of cold and darkness, with obscure noises and shadowy figures slinking at the edge of sight. And then… nothing.

CHAPTER 9

Biting the Air

The first thing I'm aware of is the smell. It is a peculiar, musty scent like fresh mulch. There are hints of flowers, and a faint tang that reminds me of coffee. The next moment I catch a whiff of a strong, sharp odor like ammonia and I choke and sputter. After a time the odor fades, allowing me to breathe again. It dawns on me that I must have been unconscious. For how long, I'm not sure.

I shift a bit. This makes me aware of the pain. The first is a sharp jab in my upper back. After that it's my right elbow and shoulder, and then my left hip. Every time I move, even if it's just my little pinkie, a new ache clamors for attention. My body must be one gigantic bruise.

I'm also soaked. My clothes cling uncomfortably to my skin. Water drips from my hair and trickles down my cheek. Strange, though, that I'm not cold.

I lie as still as possible to avoid awakening new avenues of pain. Searching my memory, I try to make sense of where I am and what's happening. I recall events in Victoria and life aboard the *Aurora*. This isn't helping. I try to release these conscious thoughts and let my mind drift.

It doesn't work. My mind is blank. The pain makes it hard to think. I shift a bit, to take the weight off my right shoulder where the worst of it is centered. The sharp pain recedes like an outgoing tide. Slowly, my mind relaxes with relief.

It comes to me in a flash: the wall of water; Dad's stricken face; endless tumbling; biting cold; desperation to breathe. A flood swept me from the cave. Where I've ended up is a mystery. I'm no longer in the water, though. Of that much I'm certain.

It's time to find out where I am, and what the situation is.

My eyes snap open. At first, this doesn't seem to make any difference. Everything is still as black as can be. But I slowly become aware of a faint glow – just the dimmest of glimmers – and in this I start to make out vague shapes. I don't seem to be outside. It's also not the cave or the lander.

As my eyes start to adjust, and the fog in my mind clears, the environment slowly reveals itself. I'm lying on a bed of what looks like leaves. There are several large tubs lined up along the wall to my right. Something weird and twisted lies on top of one of them. Gazing past my toes, I can just make out a cage. Beyond that is the source of the glow. I can't figure out what is making the light. It isn't fire; there is no flicker of flame. And it doesn't seem to be artificial. The rainbow glow has a natural feel to it.

Movement! Something large is stalking through the shadows at the very edge of the light. My heart pounds, each beat like a battering ram against my chest. I try to rise, hoping to flee, but the pain leaves me gasping for breath. There is a series of sharp clicks, like the scraping of claws against wood. My entire body tenses. I forget about my pain. I'm only aware of the death that approaches. A large shaggy face looms above me, its mouth stretched open, showing off two double rows of sharp teeth. I bite back a yelp of terror and burrow as deeply into the bed of leaves as I can. A large shadowy claw reaches out…

There is a sudden tapping on my knee. It sends an uncomfortable tingle through my body. Is the beast teasing me, the way a cat plays with a mouse it has trapped? Is it searching for the best place to slit me open? I try to draw my legs away, but the tapping continues – against my hip, against my ankle. It's somehow familiar…

A sloth-bear! That must be it. I take a closer look. Sure enough, the vague outline sharpens into the body of one of those creatures. This is a bit reassuring. They seemed friendly before… but maybe it's because they didn't think we would be too tasty. What if this one has changed its mind? Or perhaps, now that I don't have my helmet on, it doesn't realize I'm one of the beings it encountered before the storm. For that matter, is this one of the sloth-bears that were exploring the water tanks? It could be from a completely different tribe. No doubt I look like a nice, juicy meal to it. My brief feeling of comfort flees out the door, and sheer terror takes its place. I scrabble around, trying desperately to find a way to escape.

Now the creature is tapping on my shoulder and tummy. I wince as the long claws hover over my stomach. Even with my spacesuit on, one quick slash is all it would take. I wouldn't die right away; it would take agonizing minutes, perhaps even hours, to slowly bleed to death.

The tapping stops. The sloth-bear gazes intently at me. I try to relax my breathing. My lungs are pumping like runaway bellows, or like a steam locomotive charging at full speed. A moment later the sloth-bear turns and ambles away. This isn't all that comforting. I'm still trapped in an unknown place on an alien planet.

Forming an escape plan absolutely has to be my top priority, but my mind is sluggish. The only things I can think about are the large, powerful creature across the room, the aches in my body – which have returned in a rush – and my hunger. After generating numerous scenarios in which I become the sloth-bear's meal, my exhausted brain does the logical thing – it goes into sleep mode.

———

When I wake up, the sloth-bear is sitting beside me. It has something in its claws. As I watch, the sloth-bear scratches, twists, and pulls at the object. For some reason the sight makes me think of Mom, sitting in a rocking chair in our apartment in Victoria, knitting, or sewing, or fixing some small appliance. The sloth-bear is growling softly; once more I'm reminded of Mom, humming as she worked. I shake my head. I'm making everything the creature does look like a human activity. That's just silly. Whatever it's doing is completely different from what I might think it is.

The sloth-bear evidently hears the small movement of my head. It stops growling and peers around at me. I stare back, trying hard to feel confident.

A loud clatter draws my attention toward the light source. Two more sloth-bears are approaching. These are a lot smaller than the one by my bed. They rub against each other as they walk, and occasionally give little shoves.

One of the creatures comes right up to my bed and sniffs the boots of my suit. The large sloth-bear cuffs it on the side of the head, and then taps several places on the smaller creature's body. Giving me a glance that's both curious and sheepish, the small sloth-bear retreats. Its companion taps a pattern on the large sloth-bear, and then it too turns around and disappears into the darkness.

I watch all of this in silence, thinking again about how similar these actions are to those of animals on Earth. Those must be cubs. And this one is, what? Mother? Father? I decide to think of her as the mother.

The creature sets aside the object in her paws, pads to the other side of my bed on all four feet, and dips a paw into one of the tubs. Turning, she gently places something in my hands.

It feels smooth and hard, and looks like a large piece broken off a pottery bowl. A moment later I give a little yelp as she reaches for my face. Each half of her paw is as large as my head, and her claws are at least five inches long. This is it. This is the end, I think in despair. I close my eyes, waiting for the awful pain…

And feel a gentle tapping on my nose, and then my lips, and then my nose again. My eyes pop open. The sight isn't any less terrorizing. Her claws are still barely an inch from my face.

My nose starts to itch. I try to ignore it. If I move at all, I might accidentally cut myself on her claws. Or she might think

I'm attacking her and decide to take a swipe at me that *isn't* so gentle.

After several petrifying seconds, she draws her paw away and moves it toward her own face. I figure she is going to tap on her nose and lips the way she did on mine. But instead, she puts the paw to her mouth, and her teeth slice downward as she takes a bite of the air. She looks intently at me, as if trying to read my mind. Why is she biting the air? Is she insane?

A moment later, she does it again: the sloth-bear brings her paw to her mouth and bites the air. And suddenly, I feel like a complete fool. She is trying to communicate! That series of taps must mean eat, or perhaps food.

I look back at what she gave me. Should I try to eat it? What if it makes me sick like Kartak? There isn't any sickbay here, or anyone to help me get better. It's an even bigger risk than we took in eating the meat.

On the other hand, I have to eat *something*.

I try to break off a chunk. Nothing happens. Turning onto my side, I try again, putting as much force as I can into the action. One corner snaps off like a bar of chocolate breaking in two. Can I even chew this? It seems too hard. Hesitantly, with a feeling of dread causing my nerves to prickle, I place the bit in my mouth.

It softens up immediately. I find I can chew it. The food has no taste that I can detect, except perhaps a hint of bean flavor; although, that might just be my imagination.

The sloth-bear snuffles and taps me several times. I get the impression she's pleased. A feeling of pride spreads through me. I didn't need the computer to translate for me. I figured out her meaning all on my own.

The sloth-bear watches me closely. I place an edge of the food into my mouth, let it soften, and bite off another chunk. She snuffles and taps some more. I can't understand what she's saying but, gnawing on my dinner, I resolve to figure it out.

———

A loud shriek jerks me awake. Something… no, two somethings, are snarling at the foot of my bed. I watch their silhouettes, snapping, and clawing, and shoving each other. Some kind of predator must be invading the house. Could a strong-jaw climb up here? The thought gets my adrenaline pumping. They're going to tear each other apart, and me along with them!

I scrunch my legs up to get as far away from the beasts as possible. There's a loud crash, and something clatters to the floor. Now the creatures are locked together so tightly that they look like one enraged beast. The snarls make my blood freeze.

Suddenly, one of the creatures backs away. I see it in profile – it's one of the cubs! A moment later their mother trots up, growling, and gives each cub a cuff that sends it sliding across the floor.

My pulse is racing, and I realize I've climbed halfway out of the nest. I take a slow breath as it dawns on me that the two cubs have been wrestling for fun. As I slither back down into my nest, I wonder: why did they have to do it right next to me, and scare me out of my wits? They could have done it in their own space.

Then it suddenly makes sense. They probably saw that their mother was busy on the other side of the house, and wanted to show off. It's their form of Stratagem, and the cubs wanted to give a grand performance. I lie back and smile as I imagine sitting in Dead Man's Theater with a crowd of sloth-bears, watching the two cubs wrestle in the vacant lot.

Now that the cubs are quiet, I can hear the wind howling past the house. The wind is obviously powerful, yet the weaver bird house barely sways. These guys sure know how to build!

The sound makes me drowsy. I feel my eyes closing again…

CHAPTER 10

Flatbread

I have no way of tracking time. How long have I been with the sloth-bears? Several days? A week?

My body doesn't ache quite as badly. I'm determined to get up and move a little, which is a good thing. I'm sure the waste tank in my suit is getting full. So are my bladder and bowels.

Rolling onto my right side, I push myself up with my arms. It's difficult, and painful… but there; I've made it into a sitting position. A snuffling and scraping tells me that Mother is coming. The large sloth-bear probably heard me stir.

She lumbers into view as I wait for the dizziness to pass. The two cubs are right behind her, shoving each other and baring their teeth in a playful manner.

I gather my strength and slowly, shakily rise to my feet. Mother snuffles and taps me several times, showing joy at what I've done. The ceiling is low for Mother, but I have plenty of clearance.

It feels good to be standing, despite the pain and shaky muscles. Fumbling around in the dim light, I search for the clasps of my suit. I remove the gloves first, and stuff them in a large thigh pocket. Next I wiggle my arms out of the sleeves, and then slide the suit down my body. The sloth-bears watch in fascination. If the ring planet has something like snakes, they might think I'm shedding my skin.

Leaving the suit in a crumpled heap beside my bed, I take a few shuffling steps forward. Mother squeezes against the wall to let me pass. There is a circular glow in the floor up ahead. I decide to drop to my hands and knees – I don't trust my muscles yet; they might betray me at the wrong moment, and send me plunging out of the house. I crawl forward another yard or so and find myself at the edge of the exit hole. The rush of water reaches my ears. We must be above a river, perhaps the same river I saw on my first day on the planet.

Dropping my shorts, I squat by the hole and let my bowels unclench. Hopefully I'm sticking out far enough so that nothing will smear against the exit. I use a bit of my nest to wipe, empty my bladder, and decide I've had enough exercise for the moment. Pulling my shorts back up, I crawl to my bed and collapse into the nest of leaves.

Hmm. Without my suit to protect me, the nest is a bit prickly in places. I wiggle around, trying to find a position that's comfortable.

Mother approaches and taps me. Apparently it's time for another language lesson. So far, I've learned the taps for 'eat/food', 'drink/water', 'rest', 'beautiful' (I think, I'm not entirely sure I got the interpretation right on that one), showing joy, 'light', and 'no' (I get this one a lot whenever I try a new phrase). What will I learn this time?

It's slow, difficult work. Mother gives me a series of taps, and then pantomimes something. I have to figure out what she's pantomiming.

What makes it even more challenging, is that I've discovered that *where* on the body I tap is important. This makes me uncomfortable. What if my tap is off by an inch or two, and instead of saying, "Your daughter is beautiful," I say, "He smells like rotten fish?" Not only would that be embarrassing, but if I offend my hosts in such a way, it could be dangerous.

Mother gives two slow taps to my hip, three quick ones to my elbow, and another slow tap to my hip. After that she walks slowly toward the exit, then returns and looks at me expectantly. What could this pattern mean? Move? Walk? Walk slowly? Pace? Leave?

She gives the pattern again, and then walks in a small circle. So it isn't leave, and probably not pace. I decide that for now I will think of it as move/walk. Does it have to be on all fours, or could it also mean walking on two feet?

Uncertain whether my muscles will respond, I grab a bin and try to pull myself up. Somehow, I manage to rise to my feet. Still holding the bin with my left hand, I try the pattern on Mother. After giving the taps, I slowly shuffle a few steps away from my bed and back. Mother gives a bark and taps *no*.

"Okay, let's try again," I say to myself. I tap the pattern she showed me. This time, I drop down and crawl. Snuffling, Mother gives me the taps that indicate joy. So this tapping pattern means to walk on all fours.

I practice it a couple more times to lock it into my brain, and then we move on to another pattern. As she teaches me, we wander through the house. The cage I saw the first day holds a small animal. Is it just a pet, or does it serve a purpose? Continuing on, I see that the glow which lights the house comes from a large, soft mass. Could it be some kind of glow worm? A sponge? I'm not sure, but I'm confident it is some sort of living creature.

Beyond the exit hole is the sloth-bears' sleeping area. There are two nests similar to mine, and two smaller mats. I'm shocked to see that one of the larger nests is occupied. I have only met one adult sloth-bear at a time. I had assumed it was the same one, but perhaps I've been interacting with two different creatures.

The cubs are in a corner by their sleeping mats, batting a trio of ball-shaped objects to each other. Mother growls and takes a step forward. The cubs shrink away and quickly return the balls to their resting places. With that game spoiled, they turn to a large lattice against the wall. I watch in fascination as they sit and add various rods to the lattice; it appears to be some kind of toy for building structures! I watch them for a few minutes, and then my eyes take in various other objects strewn about the cubs' sleeping area.

Mother taps another pattern on my body and turns to head back. Does that mean come? I try to remember where and how she tapped, and file the information away for later use.

We return to my bed. I settle down in the leaves. Now I truly am exhausted. Even that little trip was enough to wear me out.

Sometime later I'm aware of a new sound. I realize I've been asleep. Sitting up and turning toward the sound, I see both of the adult sloth-bears sitting hunched over, facing each other, with a large object between them. The one nearest me lifts up something that looks like a leaf and places it on the object between them. The sloth-bears begin moving in a steady rhythm: one rocks backward, the other rocks forward, and then they rock the other way. This is what's creating the noise that woke me up. I crawl toward them and see that they are working together to slide a large object back and forth. Another leaf is added, this one a different shape from the first one... they're grinding them! That's what it is. There is a strong scent in the air, like the herbs Wiggs uses in his cooking.

Now that I can see the two bears together, I realize that the farther one is larger, with fur almost twice as long as its companion. The nearest one is definitely the one who has been taking care of me. I decide to continue calling her Mother in my mind (not my mother, of course, but mother to the cubs), and I'll call the other one Father.

After a while the grinding stops. Father leans forward and removes the top stone – the one they were moving. Mother scrapes the ground leaves from the bottom stone and carefully slides the flour into a small tub. Another whole leaf is placed on the large stone, and the grinding continues.

Eventually the tub is full of ground leaves. Father heaves the stones – I can't believe he can carry both at the same time – to another location in the house, while Mother reaches out a paw, gently pushes me back, and grabs a large bowl from the tubs by my bed. I watch as she dumps the leaf flour into the bowl, adds several ingredients (including some kind of liquid), and mixes them together. Growling softly, she then grabs the bowl in one paw and ambles toward the center of the house. Curiosity gets the better of me. Ignoring all my aches and pains, I crawl after her.

She stops beside the glowing creature. I notice the larger stone has been set against the wall here. The sloth-bear grabs a handful of the leaf mixture, pats it into a flat shape, and lays it on the stone, then carefully adds another two flat circles beside it.

That done, she picks up a long, odd-shaped object and starts scratching, twisting, and pulling at it. Again I'm reminded of my mom, sitting in our apartment in Victoria, working on her knitting. I settle down with my back against the wall, wondering what is going to happen to the circles of leafy mixture.

A piercing snarl causes my heart to skip a beat. My eyes search frantically for the source. It doesn't take long to track down the noise: the cubs are wrestling again, growling, batting, tumbling, knocking things over. Mother gives them a weary look, but then returns to her work. Father is doing something near his nest.

It seems like hours before Mother checks on the leaf patties. She sniffs, apparently satisfied. Carefully running a claw under each one, she lifts them from the stone and stacks them on a nearby tub. She forms and places three more flat circles onto the stone, and resumes her 'knitting'.

What's happening to the patties? They aren't cooking – there isn't any fire. Is there a chemical process going on between the different ingredients, or are they merely drying? I can't wait to try them – I'm assuming they're some kind of food. My stomach agrees; it gives a loud growl, its way of complaining about how empty it is.

As I wait, I lean back and close my eyes. My mind wanders to my dad, Kartak, and Roberts. What are they doing right now?

This gets me thinking about something that's been on my mind the past few days. I don't know where on the planet I am, or how to get back to the cave. My dad and the others don't know I'm alive. It's very unlikely I'll ever see them again.

The thought makes me feel hollow inside. The sloth-bears are nice, and I'm glad to have this chance to get to know them and learn their language. But they aren't human. I have no one to talk to, no one to laugh with. It makes me feel utterly alone.

Tears start to squeeze out between my eyelids. What will I do? What will it be like to live here, alone, for eighty, ninety, maybe even a hundred years? I won't have any technology or comforts of home. Should I spend my life exploring the planet? That would give me something to do. Or should I stay here, with the companionship of the sloth-bears? Neither future is appealing without people to share it with.

My thoughts are interrupted by a gentle tapping. *Food/eat*, Mother says. I open my eyes and find that she's offering me a piece of flatbread. I sniffle, angrily swipe the tears from my cheeks, and accept the food.

My grasp of their language isn't strong. I have to make sure I've understood correctly before I start munching. After all, it might be a rag for me to bathe with, and poisonous to eat. It would be foolish to die because I don't confirm what I think Mother said.

It doesn't take long. As soon as the cubs are given a piece, they begin devouring it at once. My stomach gives another loud growl. That's all the confirmation I need!

I tear off a piece with my teeth. The flatbread is a little stringy, and tastes like a tortilla made from a blend of cassava, corn, and dried oregano. It's a bit bland, but my stomach doesn't care. It eagerly greets the food with a low rumble that almost sounds like a purr.

As I chew, I once again consider the fact that I probably won't ever see another human again. The sloth-bears are my family now. I must accept this. Despite their kindness, they aren't the family I would choose – especially not Father. However, they are all I have. This means I have to become fluent in their tapping language. Trying to communicate with them is already making my head spin. Yet somehow, I must concentrate harder on my lessons and learn faster!

———

Mother is cleaning the 'kitchen' area. I watch as she uses a clump of some plant that looks like seaweed to wipe down the bins, grinding stones, and other surfaces. A steady pounding on the roof tells me the hail has started up again.

There's a sudden pressure on my upper arm. A quick glance reveals that Curious is gripping me with his right forepaw. *Come. Play*, the sloth-bear cub taps.

Yes, I tap back, and follow him to his sleeping mat. Timid, his brother, is sitting in a corner with his back to us.

Curious does a somersault on his way back to his sleeping area, making me laugh. The little sloth-bear is so care-free, his energy and enthusiasm are infectious. I almost copy him, but then decide I would probably end up kicking something over, or even knocking something out the exit. That wouldn't go over too well with my hosts. Instead, I stay on my feet, but I move with more of a skip than a walk.

Curious grabs the lattice and brings it to his bed. Curious and Timid have shown me how to add to the lattice. I've helped them with it a couple of times. It's not nearly as fun as Stratagem or gaming, but it's something to do. I grab a few of the long, thin strips which are pliable enough to mold into different shapes, and get to work. I still haven't figured out exactly what it is we're supposed to be building, so I just add my pieces at random. Curious doesn't seem to care.

I've only added four new strips to the structure when Curious taps *stop*. Nothing seems to hold his attention for very long. I wait as he returns the lattice to its place against the wall and grabs one of the balls. I see Timid peek around at us. Does he want to join in? I'm about to ask when I catch a glimpse of the ball whizzing toward me. Curious tossed it when I wasn't looking.

I lunge forward to grab it. The ball glances off my palms. It's heavy. The weight of it pushes my hands back. I scramble for a moment, trying to get a grip on it. Curious is snuffling with laughter at my fumbling attempts. Again the ball slips through my fingers, and this time I know there's no way I'm going to secure it. I see where it's headed and make another desperate grab for it, feeling a sense of dread. I don't even come close to capturing it.

The ball hits Father in the stomach. The great sloth-bear gives a low growl as he awakes from his slumber. Before I know it, a large arm comes swinging toward me. The backhand blow sends me flying backward. I land hard, scramble desperately to avoid falling out of the exit hole, and then lie on the smooth floor, feeling stunned. Father has never cuffed me before, and I haven't seen him cuff anyone that hard. What did I do to deserve it? I wasn't the one who threw the ball.

I feel along my chest with my hand, wincing at the pain. I hope no ribs are broken. I'm a long way from the nearest sickbay.

Mother comes and lifts me to my feet. Giving a low growl in Father's direction, she leads me to my nest. *Lie down/rest*, she taps.

I ease my body down, trying hard to ignore the pain in my chest. Mother sits beside my bed, tapping different patterns on my skin, being careful to avoid my chest. She seems to understand that it hurts.

I try to concentrate on what she's teaching me. It's difficult, because my mind keeps replaying the wallop Father gave me. One thing's for sure: I'm never going near him again!

CHAPTER 11

Unexpected Journey

Curious and Timid are fighting. Again. Although Curious is the smaller of the two sloth-bear cubs I'm living with, he isn't afraid of anything. He always has to be in control. Timid usually hangs around in the background. Today, however, they are teaching me a ball game. Timid wants to teach me the rules. So does Curious. Thus, the wrestling match.

I back away, careful to stay clear of their claws and teeth. Curious seems to have a superior position; he has a firm hold of the fur on Timid's back, and his weight is resting on his brother's neck. Perhaps this is why the fur on Timid's back is always sitting the wrong way; Curious is on Timid's back so often when they wrestle, the direction of Timid's fur has been permanently changed as a result.

I can't help taking sides. Timid usually backs down. I want to see him emerge victorious for once, in the hope that it will boost his self-confidence. I let out a chuckle and cheer him on silently, even as his plight grows even worse.

A quick twist and pull, though, and the situation is reversed. Now Timid appears to have the upper hand, using his greater size to his advantage. I have to smile at the sight of Timid being aggressive. Come on, keep it up!

The wrestlers pause for a moment, to size up the situation and plan their next move. As they become silent, my ears pick up a scraping sound behind me. I turn in time to see Father's head pop out of the entrance hole. The sharp stench of ammonia hits my nostrils. I fall against the wall, gagging. It takes my entire focus just to draw a breath.

Father emerges fully from the hole, water dripping from his long shaggy fur, and immediately starts hooting and tapping vigorously on Mother's skin. I back away from him quickly, retreating to my corner of the house. It's been at least a week since he hit me, but I haven't forgotten it! I watch him tap Mother. I don't know the language well enough to follow what he's saying, but he's definitely excited about something.

Mother waits for him to finish, and then taps back. I recognize the pattern for 'no' and the pattern for 'food/eat'. Father grunts, swats her hand away, and starts tapping furiously again. Mother sits patiently, waiting for him to finish, and then repeats what she said before. Whatever Father is saying, she is clearly standing her ground.

I can see Father's frustration. He growls, gives Mother a backhanded cuff, and stalks away. Something bumps into me from behind, nearly knocking me off my feet. Glancing down, I see Curious amble by. The discussion between the two adult sloth-bears has obviously driven wrestling from his mind. I guess that means I won't be learning the ball game just now.

Wondering what has made Father so excited, I follow Curious over to Mother. She taps something on the cub's body, and then turns to me. *Come, eat/food*, she taps.

What's happening? We just ate a little while ago. We shouldn't be eating again for a couple of hours, and I'm not really that hungry. I want to ask what Father said, but I know I won't understand the answer. I also don't want to upset Mother.

With curiosity chewing its way through my insides, I accept a piece of 'pottery bark' and two small fruits from Mother, and sit down on the edge of my bed. As I munch, I try to reason out what could be happening.

Perhaps he spotted a group of predators, and we need to eat early so we can flee. And if it's a predator that can climb up to the weaver bird houses and overpower a sloth-bear, it's definitely something to be afraid of. Or there might be another sloth-bear tribe preparing to attack, and we need to be ready to fight.

Then another idea pops into my head and makes me freeze in terror. What if the river has risen, and the house is going to get flooded? Images flash through my mind: the wall of water; the breath-stealing smack of its impact; the deep chill; tumbling out of control; banging against rocks and fallen trees; unable to breathe…

I suddenly realize my chest feels empty of air. I'm breathing, but my breaths come in short, sharp gasps that don't seem to do any good. I can't catch my breath!

A large, warm arm wraps around me. The long fur feels soft against my cheek. A deep rumble vibrates against my back and side. The effect is almost magical: a deep sense of peace comes over me and I feel my muscles relax. Soon I'm breathing normally. This is what it feels like to be held in a warm, loving embrace. Something I haven't experienced since before Mom died.

I feel a slight hitch in my breathing at the memory of Mom. But still I'm held in that firm, loving embrace, and for once the sorrow doesn't overwhelm me. I reach up my hand and stroke the furry arm that holds me. The mother sloth-bear snuffles; her arm loosens just a bit, but she continues to hold me close.

Here is a marvel. The sloth-bear is an alien, and yet she has adopted me as her own. I must look quite strange to her: small, skinny, and hairless, and yet she gives me the same love and care and protection that she gives her own cubs. How many humans would do this, even for another human? Mom and Mrs. Eldbert are the only people from Victoria that I can think of. I'm sure there are others, but not many. And how many of those would do the same for a bizarre-looking alien?

Mother continues to sit and hug me long after I've finished eating. It feels good, but my legs are starting to fall asleep. What will she do if I try to move? I don't want to hurt her feelings.

I have barely finished thinking this when the pressure is gone from my chest. I feel a gentle push in the back as Mother helps me stand up. Could the sloth-bears have some telepathic ability? This hasn't occurred to me before. But it seems like too much of a coincidence that she released the embrace right as I was thinking about it. It's something I shall have to consider, and perhaps see if I can find a way to test the theory.

Mother taps *go* onto my skin. I turn to face her, wishing I knew the tapping pattern for 'I don't understand.' Where does she want me to go?

After gazing at me for a few seconds, Mother again taps *go*. I gaze intently into her eyes, searching for any clue I can about the word. What could she possibly mean? Does she want me to play with Curious and Timid?

Giving a short growl, Mother ambles to the other side of the house. I follow, deciding that my guess must be correct. The cubs are each holding a ball. They follow me with their eyes as I approach. But Mother doesn't go to the cubs. Instead, she grabs one of Father's forelegs and pulls him toward me.

"No," I say out loud, shaking my head. I don't want to get near him!

I suddenly remember Father's agitation from before, and my heart starts to thud. Are we going out to fight? How could I possibly help in a battle? I don't know how to climb, I don't have sharp claws or long teeth, I am completely weaponless...

Mother brushes past me. I want to ask her what's going on, but I don't know how.

She returns a moment later with my wadded-up spacesuit. She shoves the suit into my arms, and then very gently takes my left hand in one of her gigantic paws and places it against Father's chest. I shrink back, waiting for him to strike. He's sitting up, the top of his head scraping the ceiling. He doesn't make any move to knock me away. This doesn't make me feel much better; he could change his mind in a flash and send me flying across the room. I look at Mother, completely bewildered. Am I supposed to pet him?

Growling, she quickly taps a pattern on Timid. Before she's even finished, he grabs a handful of Mother's fur and pulls himself up against her chest.

I'm supposed to *ride* on Father. I look up doubtfully into his face. Is this his idea or hers? What if he doesn't really want to lug me around? And then I remember the suit I'm holding. Mother must understand that I need it to keep warm outside.

I start to pull it on. The suit seems even stiffer than normal. It's been a long time since I wore it. The fabric pinches and pulls and chafes my skin and sits awkwardly on my shoulders. I'm tempted to pull it off, but the cold air will bite worse than the suit. It's something I'll have to endure.

I'm dressed, but I'm not ready. I stand, staring at the sloth-bear in front of me. It really doesn't seem wise to go grabbing the fur of such a huge creature. What if I tug at a sensitive spot by accident?

Mother isn't going to let me get out of this, though. She steps forward, grabs both of my hands, and sets them against Father's chest. I feel the slow, steady thud of his heartbeat. At least, it feels like a heartbeat. Perhaps sloth-bears have something completely different than a heart. I'm not a xenobiologist.

I scramble desperately to grip his torso with my legs as Father drops to all-fours. If I slip off now, I will fall to the floor on my back.

Hugging tightly to Father's chest, I get a whiff of his fur. This was the source of the awful stench of ammonia from before. It's much fainter now, but still powerful enough to make my stomach heave.

A moment later, though, I forget completely about the sharp odor as we lurch forward. My legs start to slip and it takes all my strength to hold on. And then my heart nearly leaps from my chest as we plunge head-first out the exit. I see the dizzying, terrifying sight of raging water below. It's much closer than it should be, assuming this is the same canyon we saw when we first landed – the rain has swollen the river to many times its normal depth. If I fall in there, I won't be coming back up.

My legs are slipping. I cling desperately to his fur with my hands. After a moment that seems to last an eternity, the sloth-bear sets out along the underside of the house. Now I'm resting on his belly, which is a tiny bit better, but not much. At least it gives me a moment to resituate myself, wrap the fur two or three times around my hands in the hope that it will help me hold on, and get a better grip with my legs.

I feel Father's powerful muscles sliding smoothly beneath me as we traverse to the canyon wall. We're getting close to the cliff…

There is a sudden jerk, and we're plunging head-first down the canyon wall. Panic grips me. I had been expecting a slight pause and a tail-first descent, which would make it easier to hold on. The abrupt change nearly tears my hands loose. And now his body is no longer supporting me. Once again there is nothing between me and a fatal plummet except my white-knuckled grip on his fur.

The thunder of water is deafening. Once more the memories crowd into my mind: the huge, powerful wave of water tearing me from the cave; getting tossed around in every possible direction; the complete disorientation; my body slamming against rocks and battered by logs; my lungs getting compressed; the deadly cold. The surface of the river is so close. Any second now, a wall of water could come and rip me away from Father.

We are halfway down. I feel myself slipping forward. Before, my head was below Father's shoulders. Now it's almost even with the top of his long neck. Remembering a horse-riding lesson from years ago, I dig in with my knees. Father gives a loud snort. Perhaps I'm hurting him, but there's no way I'm going to loosen my hold.

Father rotates as we approach the bottom, so that he descends the last few feet tail-first. The large sloth-bear seems to do this more by feel and instinct than sight. Will there be any space between the river and the cliff? What if Father has to wade at the edge of the river; will I be torn off by the current?

The roar of water grows louder with each yard we descend. The sound is overwhelming, almost like a physical assault that crashes through my entire body. At last, I see Father's rear feet set down on flat ground. He slowly squats until my feet can reach the rocky shelf. I carefully step down, one leg at a time, still clinging to his fur in case I slip. The rock shelf is about half a yard wide at this point, and less than a yard above the thundering torrent of water.

Go, Father taps against my skin. I look down at the rushing river, and cling even more tightly to his fur. I can't let go, I can't...

I feel his paws gently grasp my hands and pull. At first I don't let go. The raging water could easily overpower me. I need something solid to hold onto. Father continues to gently tug at my hands. Slowly, reluctantly, I release my grip. My legs wobble, and I grab for a hold in the cliff face. The rock is damp from the spray of water. The air still has a frosty bite to it. My hands are growing numb. It's hard for me to get a grip. My fingers might slip off the cliff face at any moment. I force myself to shuffle over the uneven surface of the ledge. It grows a bit wider, giving me the confidence to take larger strides. But then it suddenly narrows down to mere inches. I stop and look back in panic.

Father is right behind me, and to my surprise I see several other sloth-bears behind him. At almost the same time, I become aware of something else: there is a light drizzle, barely enough to dampen the skin. The horrible storm seems to be over, at least for now. This must be why Father has brought me out.

The large sloth-bear steps up to me and gently places my hands against his fur. He realizes the ledge is too narrow for me, and he's willing to give me another ride. I gratefully grab two handfuls of fur, straddle his torso with my legs, and feel the lurch as we set off together. Even though his fur is damp, it helps warm up my hands a bit.

Father climbs up a few feet, then heads horizontally. The steady pace of his legs and the rhythmic pounding of his heart are comforting. I know he won't let me fall.

We reach the end of the gorge and turn the corner. Water stretches along the cliff face. The grassy plain and part of the forest have been replaced by acres and acres of new marshland. Father continues to climb along the rock wall, swiftly and smoothly. My hands are growing tired, but I won't let them fail me. I'm going to continue to cling on for as long as it takes. We enter the trees, and still have to remain on the cliff face. Finally, the water's edge laps up against a field of mud and trees. Father doesn't put me down until we're several yards away from the swollen river. He seems to understand my terror.

The other sloth-bears gather around, seven in all. A couple of them come forward and sniff my spacesuit. It stinks, even to my unsensitive nose. That's not surprising, considering it hasn't been washed in over a month. What do they read from my smell? Do they think Father and Mother are foolish for helping me out? I can't read their expressions or follow the rapid patterns they tap.

We don't linger here for long. Father is already pacing away from the cliff, heading parallel to the river. I have to trot to keep up. We march through a woodland that has been devastated. Only half of the trees remain standing, and even some of those are leaning dangerously. I follow close behind Father, watching as he uses his great strength to push branches, and sometimes even whole trunks, out of the way. With each step I have to pull my foot from the mud with a wet *thwuck*.

Without Father's warm fur wrapped around my hands, the chill is getting to me again. Pulling my hands into my sleeves, I ball them into fists to keep them as warm as possible. My gloves are awkward. I don't want to put them on. This will keep me warm enough for now.

After an hour or so of walking, we exit the trees onto a wide field of grass. My boots feel like they weigh twenty pounds each. I search around for a moment. That will do. Plodding over to a large branch, I scrape the bottoms of my boots against it, trying to clear as much mud off as possible.

It doesn't take long for my boots to feel much lighter. Feeling pleased with myself, I look up and realize the sloth-bears haven't stopped; they are a good thirty yards away, and continuing their steady pace.

"Hey, wait up!" I shout, and jog to catch up, watching my footing carefully. These boots definitely weren't made for rough, muddy terrain. There's a lot of storm debris on the ground, mostly shattered branches. I don't want to take a wrong step and wrench my ankle.

It takes me a few minutes to close the gap. I slow to a brisk walk, and look at the massive bodies of the sloth-bears ahead of me as they trudge along in silence. Where are we going? It's clear there isn't an attack, and we don't seem to be hunting or collecting food.

Before long, we reach a broad stream of water trickling into the main river. Fortunately, it is only about ankle-deep. Before the storm, this would have been a lush meadow. We wade quickly across.

An hour or more later, Father finds two bushes growing at the base of a large pinnacle of rock. He picks several small fruits, which somehow managed to survive the ravages of the storm. I watch as he uses a long claw to split each of them open. He demonstrates scooping and eating the pulp, then hands me a couple of the fruits.

I taste a small piece of the flesh and feel my mouth instantly pucker up. It's sour! However, I like sour things, so I continue eating. Soon my tongue feels thick and my mouth dry and fuzzy, as it normally does after eating something sour. This doesn't bother me; I finish both fruits and toss the rinds to the ground. Father sees this, gives a little moan, and sets off again.

A little more rest would be nice. My legs are aching. I haven't hiked like this – or done any sort of exercise, for that matter – in a long time. And slogging through stretches of mud, like back in the forest and alongside the brook, is a lot harder than walking on the deck of a spaceship or the rocky floor of the cave. But I know I'll never convince Father to take a longer break. The only option is to keep trekking.

The ground starts to slope upward slightly. Off in the distance, I see a long shoulder of land, like a crumbling step. Is that our destination? Or is this journey going to take several days? I hope it doesn't. I want to get to where we're going, finish our mission, and get back to the sloth-bear's house. Now that the storm is over, I need to gather food and start searching for the lander. I don't want to waste too much time on whatever this is we're doing.

It takes much longer than I expect to approach the shoulder of land. It's also much taller than I thought at first glance. Now we're getting close. There is a sweet fragrance in the air. I suppose it smells like flowers, although I only know what roses and lavender smell like, and this is different.

As I slowly gaze around, drinking in the scents, I suddenly spot a dark blotch in the escarpment to my right. Could it be? I hurry forward, stumbling a bit as my gaze is fixed on the black splotch. It is a cave! But is it the right one?

I turn to ask Father, and realize that he's not beside me anymore. All seven of the sloth-bears have turned and are loping quickly away. I stand for a moment, stunned. They are moving too fast for me to catch up. They obviously intend to abandon me here, alone, with nothing to eat and no idea where I'm at. Father isn't even going to say goodbye! I've spent the last several weeks with him and his family, and now he's acting as if I'm not even here. Yes, I want to search for the lander, but I'm not ready. I need food, and planning.

Evidently, the sloth-bears don't think so. They don't give me the chance to prepare. Instead, they dump me here. I've been abandoned. I'm on my own. The thought is terrifying.

But I will survive.

CHAPTER 12

Rafiki

A mewling sound breaks into my thoughts. I ignore it. My eyes follow the sloth-bears as they grow smaller and smaller in the distance. This abrupt departure has thrown me off balance. It is taking my mind some time to adjust to this twist, to accept that it's real. I'm going to miss Mother, Timid, Curious, and yes, even Father. I can't believe I didn't even get to say goodbye to them!

Now what do I do? If this *is* the right cave, and the lander is still here, then things will be okay. If this isn't the right cave, or if the lander has left, then I'm all alone without any food. And if the lander has left, I might not even be able to tell if it's the right cave. Am I doomed to spend the rest of my days searching for a lander that may or may not still be here?

The mewing grows louder. It's an utterly pitiful sound. Gazing around, I spot movement up against the cliff wall. It's a creature about the size of my hand. I kneel down to get a closer look. I can see it shivering, and it seems to be crying. Is it a baby that's lost its mother?

"Here, I've got you," I say gently, as I scoop it up and cuddle it close. "You're okay now."

The mewling stops. I hear it snuffling, and feel gentle vibrations against my skin. I decide right away that I'm going to keep it. If the lander is gone and I'm all alone, it will be nice to have some company. And if, by some miracle, the others are still here – and if this is the right cave – then I can sneak the little guy aboard. The captain will be furious if he finds out, but it would be worth it to have the company.

It's not hard to come up with a name. He's going to be my friend. I'll call him Rafiki.

I stroke Rafiki's head as I edge toward the cave opening, my ears alert for the slightest sound. I don't have any way of defending myself against strong-jaws. My eyes scan the cliff-face. If I detect any sign of the creatures, my only hope will be to climb. It looks difficult, but I think I can manage.

I pause at the edge of the entrance. It's important to conserve the battery in my suit, but at the same time I need to use the lamp to scout the cave. I plan in my mind how I will proceed, so that I can cover the area in the shortest amount of time possible.

It's time. I steel my nerves, take one last listen, and slip around the corner, activating my lamp as I go. Right away I realize something's wrong. The cave looks different. It seems narrower, the walls more uneven than the one we landed in. Is this just a trick of my memory? Despite my uncertainty I stride forward, sweeping my lamp back and forth across the width of the cave as I walk. There aren't any animals. There's also no sign of the lander.

Soon I have all the confirmation I need. There's a wall at the rear of the cave instead of a tunnel. This isn't the right one.

I quickly return to the entrance and shut off my lamp. Now what? I must find the right cave soon. Now that the weather is good, the lander could leave at any time. The longer it takes me to find the cave, the less likely it is that the lander will still be there.

The task seems impossible. The cave could be anywhere within a hundred square miles of here. I can't search that whole area on foot, without food.

I can't think like that! I have to stay positive. I *will* find them. I just need to figure out the best plan of attack.

To the left, a waterfall plunges over the cliff like a shimmery rainbow curtain; water churns and swirls around a large caldron before reforming into the river that rushes across the plain and roars beneath the sloth-bears' house. I can't see any caves beyond the river. There could be some farther along, but crossing the wide frothing water would be next to impossible. My only hope is to follow the bluffs on this side of the river.

Realizing I'll need water, I jog to the river, wiggle my bottle out of its sleeve inside my suit, and fill it up. I take a few sips from the straw. The water is cool and fresh. I take a few more sips, fill the bottle back up, and return it to my suit. As I walk I must keep my eyes open for fruit, or maybe some of the leaves the sloth-bears fed me. I'll also need to figure out what Rafiki eats.

Before leaving, I sidle over to the cliff face, stretch my right hand out, and touch the edge of the cascading water. The main waterfall is fifty or more yards away. This appears to be a temporary offshoot created by the storm surge. The shimmery curtain is cool, and the pressure of the falling water pushes my hand down. The spray tickles my cheeks.

The sun is sinking in what I decide to call 'west'. In an hour or so it will disappear behind the top of the cliff, and this entire area will be in shadow. It's time to get moving.

I start 'southward' along the cliff, setting a steady pace that won't tire me out quickly. Most of the vegetation has been flattened by the storm, except the stuff growing right up against the cliff. This makes the going easier.

I pass the cave where the sloth-bears left me and soon find another cave. I can tell right away that it's too small, so I don't bother exploring it.

My stomach begins to grumble. None of the bushes along the cliff look promising. I don't dare eat anything I haven't tried before, except as an absolute last resort. I don't know which plants and fruit might be poisonous.

After trudging for half an hour, the vegetation changes. A leaf catches my eye. That looks like one of the types Mother used to make the tortilla! The fruit on a nearby bush also looks familiar. Excited, I slip Rafiki into a pocket and gather leaves in one hand, fruit in the other. I offer some of both to Rafiki, hoping it's something he can eat. He immediately starts nibbling on a leaf. I bite into a piece of fruit; the sweet flavor bursts into my mouth. I can't let it distract me, though. I must keep watch for caves… not to mention predators.

We finish our supper just as the sun dips below the top of the cliff. This leaves me with a decision to make. I really want to continue the search nonstop. However, it won't do any good to exhaust myself. I must remember that the search might take a week or more. Rest will be important, and on the ring planet, the shadows under the cliff are as close to nighttime as I'm going to get. And I'm tired. The adrenaline of the climb down from the sloth-bears' home has worn off. I feel a great weariness in my body and mind. I also haven't seen any creatures on my walk today. They might still be hibernating. If that's true, it would be safest to rest now, before they emerge from the cave. This helps me make up my mind. I'll take a short rest, and continue my search in a couple of hours.

It doesn't feel safe to sleep on the field of grass. It's too exposed. Instead, I burrow under the shrubbery at the base of the cliff. It's uncomfortable: the ground is hard, sticks poke into me, and damp leaves tickle my face. Now that the sun has disappeared, my body shivers and my teeth chatter. For the moment, warmth is more important than convenience. I pull on my gloves and lock them into place. I yearn for the warm comfort of my nest, with Mother snuffling beside me as she grinds leaves. I shift around, trying to get comfortable. I know I'll never fall asleep, but at least I can relax for a little while…

The next thing I know, I'm opening my eyes and my mind is groggy. Despite my discomfort, I managed to sleep.

I peek down at Rafiki to make sure he's okay. The little guy must have crawled out of the pocket while I was sleeping. He is snuggled up against my arm, his body vibrating to tiny snores.

I rise gently, being careful not to wake him. My back is sore and my muscles are stiff. I haven't had much exercise lately, and my body is letting me know it.

The sun is already bright in the sky to my left. It swept all the way below the underside of the ring planet as I slept. That's not good. I must have been asleep much longer than I wanted. I can't waste valuable time like that!

I set out at once, munching on leaves as I walk. The only sounds I hear are the ones I'm making. There's still no sign of anything stirring. I pass grottos and clefts; there's one stretch of cliff that has a long rock overhang, like a giant overbite. The land is wide and barren and empty. My feeling of loneliness grows sharper as I march on without pause.

Several dreary hours later, the terrain changes. Instead of flat grassland, there are now little water-filled gullies that cut across my path. This slows me down. Each time I come to a gully, I slip and slide down a short slope, hop across the stream at the bottom, and clamber up the far side. I'm soon hot and weary. I haven't seen a cave yet today.

The sun slides behind the upper portion of the ring, casting a broad shadow across the land. I spot a couple of bushes with berries, and another with leaves I can eat.

As I sit and munch, I wonder how much ground I've covered. Four or five miles? It hasn't been much. There's still so much land to search! The shoulder of land stretches off in the distance as far as my eyes can see.

I don't allow myself much of a break. As soon as I've eaten my lunch, I trudge onward, hoping to spot a cave.

The shadows lengthen again. Discouraged by a day of fruitless searching, I snake my way into the shrubbery at the base of the cliff. This time, sleep won't come. The ground is uneven, and I can't get comfortable. My ears prick at the tiniest sounds. Still, there is no sign of any animal lurking nearby.

After resting for a couple of hours, I drag myself to my feet and set out again. The going is slow in the dim light. I spot a couple of small caves, but nothing worth exploring.

Even the return of the sun doesn't lift my mood. The shoulder of land stretches onward, bleak and featureless. My search seems pointless. The lander must have left by now – they probably departed as soon as the weather cleared. I'll never see them again.

Taking a deep breath, I push these dark thoughts aside. I can't give up yet.

I pause my march long enough to forage for food. The pickings are slim: two tattered leaves and three small fruits. This quick snack isn't nearly enough. Ignoring my grumbling stomach, I trudge on. I must keep going as long as my strength holds out.

I've lost count of how many gullies I've stumbled in and out of, or how many streams I've hopped across. My legs feel leaden and my feet ache. My hands are scratched and dirty from clambering up slopes.

I round a slight bend in the cliff face, and my spirits lift a tiny bit. A cave looms before me. It's the largest one I've encountered so far. Switching on my lamp, I head inside. This one feels right: the dimensions, the shape of the walls and floor, the height. I hurry forward, sweeping my lamp back and forth. There is no sign of the lander. I push on, wanting to confirm that I'm in the right place. The cave narrows. However, instead of a tunnel, the cave widens again into a sizeable cavern. It's filled with sleeping creatures. Backpedaling quickly, keeping a sharp eye on the cavern entrance, I retrace my steps to the outside world and flick my lamp off.

Two hours of walking yields nothing. The sun disappears behind the bluff. The last rays sparkle on a stream that cuts across my path. Deciding to rest before conquering the stream, I find another cluster of bushes to burrow into. The endless searching and lack of sleep have left me exhausted. I stroke Rafiki's fur, trying to draw some comfort and hope from my little friend.

I wake up cold and stiff. My neck is a bit itchy. I don't feel like getting up. I know I have to keep searching, but my muscles are tired, and I want to rest a bit longer.

Rafiki is muttering and mewling, like a baby gurgling to itself. I snuggle with the little guy, trying to imagine what he must be thinking. Rafiki's squeaking grunts continue, but I slowly become aware that there is another noise that comes and goes in the background. This is what woke me up. Focusing intently on the sound, I suddenly stiffen. It's human voices!

Ecstatic, I gently pick Rafiki up and bull my way through the bushes, not caring about the scratches to my forehead and cheeks. I hurry along the cliff, eyes scanning for the cave.

There it is! The cave is the source of the stream. I rush forward, filled with excitement and relief, listening intently.

"We can't leave Sean!" I hear my dad say. His voice sounds cracked and strained.

"We have to get Roberts to sickbay," Kartak says. I wonder what has happened to the crazy old scientist? I stop just outside the cave entrance and listen. I want to hear where the debate goes.

"He's stable. He can wait a little longer," replies my dad.

"It's been almost a month," Kartak says. "I don't like it any more than you do. But even if he didn't drown right away, he didn't have any shelter, and all the animals are in here. How could he have gotten food?"

"Plants," my dad points out simply.

"Think about how big the planet is," Kartak says. "The water could have swept him anywhere. We don't have enough fuel for a search."

"We can get more from the *Aurora*. We have to try!" my dad insists. I feel a surge of compassion for him. I never thought he would stand up for me like this!

"The storm might start up again and trap us here another couple of months," Kartak retorts. "We have to leave now!"

"I'm not going without my son."

"Look, I don't want to leave you behind," Kartak says grimly. "But if you insist on staying, I will leave you here."

"You do what you must," my dad says resolutely. This has me totally flabbergasted. My dad would give up his link to humanity to search for me? It doesn't seem possible, and yet I can't imagine he's trying to bluff Kartak. Unable to contain myself any longer, I slip Rafiki into a pocket, whisper for him to keep quiet, and step into the cave. "I'm here."

The two of them turn and gape at me. My dad stumbles a bit, as if dazed, and then rushes forward and grabs me in a huge hug. "Sean," he says. "I knew you'd make it. I just knew it!"

Tears sting my eyes. The sloth-bears are wonderful, but it's great to be back amongst humans. I haven't been left behind.

My emotions burst. Tears rush down my cheeks, and my muscles feel slack. I let Dad hold me and comfort me. He isn't the strongest person, or the kindest, and he tends to make a mess of his hair and goatee, but he is my dad. I'm ready to admit that now.

CHAPTER 13

The Search

Roberts is a mess. "He went out to get firewood yesterday," Dad explains. "Two strong-jaws attacked. He was able to shoot the first one, but the second one knocked the pistol from his hand. I heard the commotion and hurried out. By the time I was able to drive the strong-jaw away, it had done this to him."

I shake my head at the sight. Roberts is lying on his stomach, wearing only a pair of shorts. His back is striped by numerous gouges – claw marks, I decide upon closer inspection. And a pair of puncture wounds in his shoulder – the strong-jaw must have sunk its teeth in there. I can't imagine how painful the wounds must be.

"Secure his legs," my dad says. "I'll handle the rest. Make sure the straps are tight."

I pull two sets of straps across Roberts' legs and cinch them until they are taut. My dad does the same with his upper body, laying thick layers of medic-foam between the belts and Roberts' back to protect the wounds. Roberts lets out a low moan as my dad tightens the last strap, making me wince. I wouldn't want to travel like that.

"Now for the meat," Dad says.

Ever since I was washed away, Kartak and my dad have been collecting meat every couple of days. Unsure of the best way to preserve it, they have decided to try several methods: cooking, smoking, salting, and freezing. There is one last haunch on the fire.

I am extra careful when we open the airlock. I don't want to end up like Roberts… or worse. And now that the storm has stopped, the animals will be stirring soon.

We sweep our lamps across the cave three times before slowly emerging from the lander. My dad walks forward. I follow, walking backward, keeping an eye out for animals that might try to sneak up from behind. I feel the heat of the fire on the back of my neck. We're close.

"Okay, I'll carry the meat," Dad says. "You put out the fire and scatter the ashes."

My dad uses two long forks to lift the haunch off the fire. He steps back and scans the cave, keeping guard while I take care of the fire. It doesn't take me long to extinguish it and scatter the ashes, but every second is nerve-racking. Is a strong-jaw eyeing us from the shadows? Is a family of the beasts creating a circle around us in the darkness, intent on trapping us away from the lander?

Finally, I'm done. "Let's go," I say, wanting only to get back to the safety of the ship.

We walk quickly, but remain vigilant. A low moan comes from the tunnel entrance, followed by a snort – that came from inside the cave! The edge of my lamp beam illuminates several legs. A cacophony of grunts, snorts, and bellows reaches my ears, and now there are several animals moving through the shaft of light from my headlamp.

"Come on, Sean!" my dad says, breaking into a jog. The noise of footfalls grows louder behind us. Will we reach the lander in time?

And then we're in the airlock, and I quickly slap the door sensor. The hatch slides shut, cutting off the building thunder of footfalls. I let out a relieved breath. Hopefully I won't have to deal with the strong-jaws again!

I help my dad lash down the hunk of meat, slice off a piece to gnaw on, and then follow him to the flight deck. "Roberts all set?" Kartak asks, without looking up from the instrument panel.

"As snug as can be," my dad replies, strapping himself into a seat. "And we brought in the last of the meat."

"Have you figured out a way to find the *Aurora*?" I ask, taking a chair near Kartak. The normal sensors don't work in this rainbow of light, so we can't use them to scan for the ship. On previous flights, the lander's computer tracked the *Aurora's* trajectory, the lander's trajectory, and the elapsed time. Kartak used these to plot a return course. Now, however, so much time has passed – plus we don't know exactly how long we've been on the planet – and the *Aurora's* trajectory is no longer known. We don't have enough data to plot a return course. *If* the *Aurora* is even still in orbit. They might have given up on us and left.

"I have a few ideas," Kartak says, still busy getting the lander ready for launch. "We know approximately how far away the *Aurora's* orbit was from the planet. I doubt they've changed it. That gives us a starting point. We also know the captain's flying style and preferences. We'll find them."

He sounds a lot more certain than I feel.

"We may as well get comfortable," Kartak says after a moment. "It's turned into rush hour out there." Swiveling his chair to face me, he adds, "And I'm anxious to hear what you've been up to the last few weeks."

"That makes two of us," Dad says.

Gazing out at the steady stream of animals illuminated by the lander's lights, I tell them about returning to consciousness, about Mother, Father, Curious, and Timid, about learning some of their language, about their house, and about the descent down the cliff and the trip back to the cave. My memories of the sloth-bears have a wistful tinge. Without them I would be dead right now, and I never had a chance to thank them for all they did.

"All right, we're green for launch," Kartak says with a crooked grin. "Here we go!"

The lander lifts smoothly off the ground. Kartak carefully rotates the craft around so that our nose is pointed toward the cave exit. The stream has become a muddy mess, churned and trampled by the mass exodus of animals. There are still a few creatures in sight, meandering across the storm-ravaged land.

The cave walls slip past the canopy, and a moment later we're out in the rainbow-colored sunlight. Kartak points the lander's nose toward space and guns the engines. It feels good to be leaving the storm planet behind.

And then the turbulence hits.

The lander is shaken like a pair of dice in someone's hand. I grip the armrests of my seat, wondering if we'll make it off the planet after all – the disc seems reluctant to release us. Kartak's mouth is a thin line, his brow furrowed in concentration.

And then as abruptly as the turbulence started, it stops. The lander flies smoothly upward, past the fringes of the atmosphere, into space.

The search for the *Aurora* begins.

I focus on the space outside the viewport, looking for any vague outline in the bright rainbow background. Compared to the vast amount of space surrounding us, the *Aurora* is small – in fact, downright tiny. I begin to realize just how nearly impossible it will be for us to find the ship. We could fly within a couple hundred yards of the *Aurora* and fail to spot it.

Dad mentioned that he and Kartak filled the air tanks. They should last us a week or so. Will we manage to find the ship by then, or will we be forced to return to the ring planet for more air? And if so, what if the storm returns?

After only five minutes, my eyes are sore from straining to catch a glimpse of the ship. How long can I keep this up? There won't be any chance to rest my eyes; if I turn away from the viewport, or close them for even an instant, I might miss the *Aurora*. Even so, I have to change tactics. I can't keep straining like this.

I keep my gaze focused out the viewport, but instead of straining to see everything, I try to relax and simply look with normal intensity. This eases the discomfort in my eyes a bit. It will have to be good enough.

———

We reach orbit and Kartak cuts the engines. Straight away, my stomach gives a heave. Remembering my last experience with zero-g, a surge of panic rises in me – I don't want to be sick in front of Dad and Kartak!

I look around desperately and spot several of those weird barf bags in a pocket to my right. Trying to appear nonchalant, I edge my right hand toward them so that it'll be ready to grab one should the need arise.

"We need to set up a sleep rotation, so that there is always someone watching up here," Kartak says. This makes sense. I really don't want to leave the search – my eyes are still the best, after all – but this would be the perfect excuse to get away from Dad and Kartak… just in case. A sudden squirming inside my pocket reminds me Rafiki is still in there – another reason to leave the flight deck.

"I'll sleep first," I say, and unbuckle myself before anyone responds. Barely able to keep my last meal down, I launch desperately through the hatchway, hoping to find more of the fancy bags before it's too late.

I glide through the cargo hold, past large chunks of preserved meat, and grab a chair as I enter the kitchenette. I fumble through three cabinets, but come up empty. Surely the kitchenette of all places would have barf bags! My eyes zoom around the little room… there! A pocket on the side of the freezer holds about a dozen bags. I grab one and place it to my mouth. Again my stomach heaves, but nothing comes up. I snatch a second bag for backup, then glide to my bunk. I slip into the large sleeve – like a sleeping bag – hold a bag at the ready, and try to relax.

It doesn't work. My stomach is still complaining, and my mind is busy thinking up possible endings to our trip: running out of air before we can return to the planet; missing the *Aurora* and returning to the planet, only to find that we don't have enough fuel to launch again; returning to the planet and getting grounded by another storm; spotting the *Aurora* just in time to see the starship turn and leave orbit.

I take Rafiki out of my pocket. The little guy is trembling. Holding him carefully so that he doesn't float away, I stroke his fur gently. He stops wiggling and I hear little moans that sound like he's pleased. I let out a little chuckle as his large round eyes stare into mine. He's a cute little thing!

Before long I start to get drowsy. I don't want Rafiki to float away, so I tuck him back into my pocket. I can feel tiny vibrations as he breathes. It tickles.

As I float in my sleeve, my mind returns to the *Aurora*. Once more I imagine various scenarios of doom. Before long I'm wide awake, my heart pounding at the thought of never seeing the ship again.

I hear my dad bang into a wall as he maneuvers through the hatchway several hours later. "Sean, are you awake?" he calls softly.

"Yes," I reply.

"Could you help me with Roberts? I want to get him into a sleeping sleeve."

"Sure," I say.

Slipping out of my bed, I glide over to Roberts' bunk. My dad and I carefully unstrap the goofy scientist. I soon find that it's not easy to guide his limp body into a sleeve. His legs keep folding up; it's like trying to slip a ragged thread through the eye of a needle.

"That was annoying," Dad says at last, once Roberts is finally snug in his sleeve.

"Not something I want to do every day," I say in agreement. "Especially without gravity."

"Thanks for your help," my dad says.

"You're welcome," I reply with a shrug. An awkward silence follows. "I'm going to the cockpit," I say after a few moments to escape the uncomfortable situation, despite the fact that I didn't catch even a short snooze. At least I haven't been sick yet, and my stomach is feeling a teeny bit better.

"I'll see you later," Dad calls after me. I mumble a reply as I glide away through the cargo space.

"No luck?" I ask Kartak, as I strap into the same chair as before.

"There's nothing out there that I can see," he replies.

I settle down to the task of scanning around us, hoping to catch a glimpse of the *Aurora*. To catch a glimpse of home.

———

"Here you go," I whisper to Rafiki, slipping him a small piece of leaf. He slides the morsel to the back of his mouth and chomps up and down. After a moment he swallows, and looks up at me with his big eyes. I smile and feed him another piece.

"What's that?" Kartak says sharply from right behind me, making me jump. I didn't hear him approach. A momentary panic grips me. My eyes scan the table; my brain runs through possible places to stash Rafiki. I'm stumped. There's nowhere I can hide the little guy, no way to disguise the sound of his tiny bites. It's best to come clean.

"I found him when I was searching for the cave," I say, holding Rafiki up so that Kartak can see him clearly. "He was lost and alone. Just like me. I figured we could keep each other company."

"He is cute," Kartak says, peering closely at the little guy. His brow furrows in thought. A moment later he lets out his breath. "He doesn't look like he eats much. I suppose you can keep him. Just don't let the captain find out when we get back."

"Thanks, Kartak!" I say, beaming. "No, he doesn't eat much at all." Then the last part of Kartak's statement hits me and I sober up. "Do you still think we'll find the *Aurora*?" I ask.

"It is taking longer than I expected, but we'll find her," Kartak replies. "It's only been three days. We can't give up hope so quickly.

"And speaking of the *Aurora*, you'd better go relieve your dad. I'm sure his eyes must be getting tired by now."

"Yeah, I guess it's time for my turn. Come on, Rafiki, let's go on watch," I say, settling the little guy on my shoulder as I position myself for launch. I feel Rafiki's tiny claws grip my shirt to hold himself securely in place. "I'll see you later," I say to Kartak, and then head toward the flight deck.

Kartak says not to lose hope, but it's hard to stay positive. Every minute that ticks by makes me that much more certain that any hope of sighting the *Aurora* is just a foolish dream. Even so, I catch myself thinking that perhaps, just this once, the dream can become a reality.

Another day lumbers by. There has been no break in the routine, nothing to interrupt the monotony of staring out the porthole, not a single thing to disrupt or distort the endless view of brilliant strips of colored light.

I have something I want to talk to Dad about, but it's awkward and uncomfortable. Every time I leave my bunk to relieve him on the flight deck, I plan to speak to him about it. By the time I reach the flight deck, I've talked myself out of it, and remain silent on the subject. Every single time. It's extremely frustrating.

This time will be different. I firm my resolve. I *will* ask him.

Pushing off from the table in the kitchenette, I glide through the cargo hold. The dented water tub is lashed down. Kartak is going to patch it up when we get back aboard the *Aurora*. The meat remains firmly in place, giving off a mixture of aromas unlike anything from Earth. I reach the door to the cockpit, grab the frame, and pause for a second. My dad is strapped down in the pilot's seat, his head turning left and right as he scans out the porthole.

It's happening again. My throat is tightening. I don't want to do this. I can't confront him.

Closing my eyes, I clench my fists and shake my head. I can't let this fear keep its grip on me. It's now or never. Opening my eyes, I glide into the cockpit and grab a seat back.

"Hi, Sean! That time already, huh?" Dad says, without taking his eyes from the porthole.

"It's that time," I manage to croak. His head turns at the sound of my voice. Before my resolve crumbles completely, I blurt, "Hey, Dad. Before you leave, there's something I need to know." Steeling my nerves, I look up and meet his eyes. "Why did you leave me and Mom?"

A twinge of pain passes across Dad's face and he looks away. He is silent for a long moment, staring out the porthole. Then, giving a deep sigh, his gaze returns to my face. "I've been expecting this question for a long time," he says hoarsely. "For years I've imagined what it would be like to face you, and try to explain it."

Again he pauses and looks away. I can read the years of turmoil in his face. A sheen of tears glistens in his eyes.

"It was a one-year mission," he explains softly. "I thought we would be going together as a family. On the evening before departure, your mom broke the news to me: she wasn't coming. She said it would be too risky for you. I was torn up inside. I didn't want to leave the two of you, but the expedition was the chance of a lifetime. And after all, it was only going to last one year. So I went.

"As soon as we left, I knew I'd made a mistake. What mattered was you and Mom, not some scientific expedition. But it was too late. We were accelerating for deep space. They couldn't waste the fuel and time to stop the flight for me. This wasn't a pleasure cruise, where I could skip ship at the first port of call. There weren't any other ships we could meet up with that could take me back to Earth. I was stuck on board for the duration of the expedition."

Dad pauses, his gaze still fixed out the viewport. He clears his throat, and then continues. "We got back to Earth a year later. I had every intention of rejoining you and Mom. I couldn't wait to see you, to hold you, to laugh with you!

"But I started having doubts. Would your mom even want to see me? Would she welcome me back, or would she reject me for leaving the two of you? As I was sitting, trying to build up the courage to board the shuttle for Victoria, one of the scientists from the expedition approached me. He told me he had just been recruited for another trip, and they were still trying to fill out the roster. I decided another year wouldn't make much difference. I left a message with your mom, saying my trip had been extended."

My chest is tight with emotion. How could Dad possibly doubt that Mom would want to see him? How could he even conceive of the possibility that she might reject him? That's just not who Mom is.

Sighing, my dad says, "What a fool I was. As time passed, it grew harder and harder to build up the courage to face Mom. Every time I returned from a trip, I desperately wanted to see the two of you. I have no excuse, Sean. I don't deserve – "

"I forgive you, Dad," I whisper. Pulling myself over to his chair, I put my arms around him.

This hasn't been an easy conversation to face. But it's something I've needed to hear for a long time. As each short segment of Dad's story has unfolded, a little bit more of my anger and resentment has drained away. I don't agree with how things unfolded, or the decisions he made, but now at least I have some understanding of it.

"Thanks for telling me," I say hoarsely, releasing him from the hug. Grabbing an armrest, I pull myself down into the chair and secure the restraints.

"You're welcome, Sean," he replies, his voice rough and gravelly. "I'm glad we've had this talk. I should have done it a long time ago. If you want to talk about it again sometime, just let me know."

"Yates, can you help me with Roberts before you turn in?" Kartak asks from behind, startling me. I turn and see him glide silently onto the flight deck and grab a chair. Twice a day we have to wiggle Roberts out of his sleeve, redress his wounds, and stuff him back into the sleeve again. I'm glad it's Dad's turn to help with this.

"You bet," my dad says, hitting his harness release and quickly pushing himself up. Squeezing my shoulder, Dad gives me a watery smile, and then glides out the door.

Still processing my emotions from Dad's story, I set my shoulders, and slowly run my eyes back and forth across the expanse outside the porthole.

———

"Anything?" I ask automatically, as I glide into the cockpit. I hardly even pay attention to the response, knowing exactly what it will be.

"Nothing but rainbow," Kartak mutters back. It appears that even his hope has almost drained dry.

"Are we going down soon?" I ask, strapping down in a seat next to where he's sitting.

"We'll give it another quarter-hour," Kartak replies, fiddling with a control.

We've been searching for about a week, and we're already pushing the limits of our air. It may only be my imagination, but the air seems to get worse with every breath I take. It's not too bad yet. Still, I don't want the atmosphere to get so bad that Kartak passes out before we land.

I stare out the cockpit viewport, not really focusing on anything. My mind drifts back to my time with the tulip people: the aliens guiding me down to the planet; rain splattering against my spacesuit helmet; flying through the rainbow with a peppermint-tasting wind blowing against my face. I would love to be there right now, soaring through space with tulip people all around me.

"That's it," Kartak says. "We have to turn back."

I slump down, all hope gone. This is it. We're doomed. The *Aurora* is gone.

Just as despair wells up inside, something catches my eye… I think. Did I just imagine it?

"Wait! What's that?" I lean forward, straining against my straps, and peer into the rainbow. Where is it?

"What's what?" Kartak asks sharply, craning his neck forward and scanning the space around us.

"I thought I saw something, but it must have been my… No! There it is!" I shout, pointing to a vague outline forming to our left.

Kartak taps the thruster controls, banks the lander slightly, and after a few seconds all doubt is gone from my mind. It's definitely the *Aurora*. "There she is," he says. Kartak turns to me and smiles. "I told you we'd make it."

I grin back. "We've found it, Rafiki!" I shout, barely even noticing how bad the air has gotten. "I'm going to tell Dad."

Before leaving the flight deck, I take one more look out the viewport. Just to make sure it's real. Nothing has ever looked so welcome and wonderful to me.

CHAPTER 14

Black Hole?

"Welcome back," the captain's voice booms through the landing bay.

"We would've felt more welcome without the 24-hour quarantine," Kartak mutters, rubbing his new, unkempt beard.

"We had to be sure –" the captain starts to say.

"You had to be sure we aren't carrying any alien diseases," Kartak says, interrupting. "I know. It still doesn't make the waiting any easier."

"Just be glad you made it back when you did," the captain says, clearly irritated at being interrupted. "We were giving you one more day before leaving orbit."

"I'm surprised you waited this long," Kartak says. "Since you didn't know about the storm –"

"But we did know." This time it's the captain's turn to interrupt. "When you were more than a day overdue, I took the *Aurora* into a lower orbit. We launched a pod, and were within range of its transmissions. It picked up the storm… or rather, I should say that the storm picked *it* up. The pod only transmitted for a few minutes before the interference got too bad. We haven't heard from it since. I'm guessing it has become a permanent resident of the planet."

"Even so, how did you know the storm would last that long?" Kartak asks.

Rafiki chooses this moment to poke his nose out of my pocket. I hastily ease him back down. Thankfully, the captain is too engaged in the conversation to notice.

"We launched a pod every three days, making sure they didn't go all the way down to the atmosphere," the captain explains. "About a week ago, we received data suggesting the storm had blown itself out. I moved the ship into a higher orbit, anticipating that's where you would be searching for us."

The captain is taking all the credit for this. Was all of it really his idea? It sounds more like something Johnson would come up with.

"We're extremely glad you waited for us," my dad says. "Right now, though, we need to get Roberts to sickbay."

"Right!" the captain thunders. "Kartak and Yates, transfer him. Make it quick!"

"Yes, sir," they reply.

Kartak fetches a hover stretcher. I walk behind them as they guide Roberts to the elevator. It's nice to be able to move more than a few yards again. The lander was feeling rather cramped toward the end of the search.

They get Roberts situated in sickbay. He's unconscious. A couple of the gashes in his back look particularly nasty – the edges are dark and puffy. It will take them a while to heal.

"Sean, could you help me get the meat to the galley?" Wiggs asks, as we mingle around Roberts' bed.

"Sure," I reply. This will allow me to stretch my legs a bit more. Plus, it will be nice to chat with Wiggs. It's been a while. "Just let me take care of my suit first."

"Of course," says Wiggs. "I'll meet you in the landing bay."

I trot to the rack room. My spacesuit needs a complete overhaul: the septic tanks need purging, the oxygen tank needs replenishing, the battery needs charging, the water bottle needs refilling, and the whole thing needs a good wash.

Rafiki climbs onto my shoulder to watch the operation. I don't mind. The captain isn't here; there's very little risk of my little friend being spotted.

My nose curls as I empty the septic tanks. I put the suit into the cleaner and set it for a long cycle. It comes out steaming. Most of the stink is gone, although I can still detect a faint whiff of stale sweat. After filling up the oxygen tank and water bottle, I place the suit on the rack and hook it up to a charger.

Rafiki seems to follow all of this with intense interest. He makes little snuffles and mews as I work. When I finish, he gives a loud snort. I smile, imagining this as a sign of approval for the incredible transformation my suit has gone through.

"Okay, time to go undercover," I tell him, and slip Rafiki into my shirt pocket. He squirms around, tickling my chest. Laughing, I head for the landing bay.

"Great work!" Wiggs says as I approach the lander. "It looks like there's enough meat here to last a month or more."

"There's some in the freeze box, too," I say. "We tried different ways of keeping the meat from spoiling."

"Hopefully it works better than the preservatives in the rations," Wiggs comments.

I hadn't even thought of that. What if the meat spoils quickly despite our efforts? We need this food!

Wiggs hands me a slab of meat and grabs a couple for himself. We haul our loads up to the galley.

"I've cleared some room in these cupboards," Kartak says when we arrive, indicating a row of storage spaces. Wiggs and I stuff our load into one of the cabinets, forcing it into as small a space as possible. Rafiki peeks his head out at the noise. I hastily nudge him back down into concealment.

"That's as good as we can get it," Kartak says, eyeing the meat. "Let's keep going. I'll help you carry the rest."

It takes four more trips to transport the meat to its new home. We have to leave the last batch out on the counter. The cupboards are bursting at the seams.

The captain sweeps into the galley as we're about to leave. With his size and energy filling up the space of several people, the moderate-sized room feels cramped.

"The freeze box is full, as are these cupboards," Kartak says, indicating the various niches where slabs of meat are lurking. "We didn't have enough room for all of it, so some will have to stay on the counter. We've preserved it, too. It should last a while."

The captain opens each of the cupboards and runs his eyes across the contents, as if he has to prove to himself that Kartak is being truthful. In the end he nods appreciatively. "Well done! This will allow us to increase our rations. I'm sure our stomachs will appreciate that. And you're absolutely certain it won't make us sick like the alien food from that other planet?"

"The four of us have been surviving off it for over a month now," Kartak replies. "We haven't had any problems."

"Very good. Excellent. The computer has plotted us a new course. This meat should give us enough food to last until we're back in our own space."

The captain is brimming with confidence as he says this. Does he really think we're going to find our way back soon, or is this just a show? If it's a show, he's a great actor. I wish I had his confidence. At this point, I would settle for making it back to our own space sometime before all the scientists turn senile. Cleaning up after Kartak when he was sick was bad enough. I don't want to have to look after grouchy old people *and* run the ship all by myself. The thought makes me shudder.

Feeling Rafiki stir in my pocket, I glance at the captain and rush out the hatch. There's no one in the corridor, so I let the little guy peek out – like a dog sticking its head out the window of a hopper – as I stride toward my cabin. He blinks and makes little grunts of pleasure. Getting a taste of freedom, he decides to push the boundaries. The little guy starts to climb up my sleeve.

"Sorry, I can't let you do that out here," I say, and ease him back down. I feel sorry about keeping him cooped up in my pocket. The instant my cabin door swishes shut behind me, I release him from his prison.

I place him on the deck. Rafiki stands there, shivering. His nose twitches. He looks cautiously around, and takes a tentative step forward.

Hopping onto my bunk, I watch as he slowly explores his new home. He stays out in the open, away from the bunk, desk, and cabinet. Does he fear a predator might be lurking out of sight?

Twenty minutes later, he stops by the bunk and looks up at me with his soft, round eyes. "What do you think?" I ask, as I gently pick him up. He nuzzles my finger. His trembling body is all the answer I need. It will take him a while to adjust to the new setting. In time, though, I'm confident he will get comfortable here. I'm glad he's with me. It will be so good to have the company!

———

Roberts is starting to look a little better. Scabs have formed, the swelling is down, and his fever is cooling. He's still only semi-conscious, but I'm confident that will soon change.

"What do you have planned for today?" Dad asks. He fiddles with one of the monitors on the other side of Roberts' bed in sickbay. The screen shimmers as the setting changes.

"I have my first appointment," I reply, holding up a set of tools for him to see. A smile creases his face at the sight. "In fact, I'd better get going."

"You definitely don't want to keep your customers waiting," Dad says, making another adjustment to the medical equipment. "Who's your first guinea pig?"

"Wiggs," I say, pausing to let the hatch open.

As I exit, I hear Dad's chortle. "Good luck with that," he shouts as the door swishes closed.

"Thanks," I mutter to myself. I have a feeling I'm going to need it.

I'm soon at Wiggs's door. I take a few breaths of clean air, and then knock.

"Is that my barber?" Wiggs calls from within.

"It is," I shout back.

The hatch opens. Wiggs's bulk blocks the entryway. He wheezes, and places a hand on the hatch frame to steady himself.

"Come in, come in," he says, pushing off from the hatch frame and waddling toward his couch. "Remember, nothing too fancy. Just a little trim would be fine."

"Got it. Just a trim."

I set down my weapons – shears, comb, spray bottle – and take a look at the battleground. This is going to be a long, grueling campaign. Examining Wiggs's hair up close only reinforces the image of a wild bird's nest: strands sticking out in every conceivable direction, snarls that have been years in the making, wiry bristles that look tough enough to break the shears. Dad's laughing face pops into my mind. He was definitely right to be amused. I'm not sure how this is going to turn out.

I start with the spray bottle, misting his hair and goatee. It's time for the comb. Wiggs closes his eyes and winces as I use short, jerky movements to attack his hair. "Ow!" he exclaims. "Easy does it, Sean!"

"If I go easy on this, I'll never get anywhere," I say grimly, continuing my mission. I feel bad about it – I can thoroughly empathize with Wiggs's pain. I glance around, trying to think of a way to take his mind off of his scalp. My eyes land on his gaming system. I recall the very first time we played on it – we couldn't see our avatars; we had to play entirely by sound. And Wiggs managed to distract me with a certain conversation topic... That would be the perfect diversion. "I've got a question," I say, flicking my eyes back to Wiggs's goatee and resuming my attack with the comb.

"Shoot," Wiggs says.

"A while back you talked about Tanzania assimilating the world. I never understood that. Why weren't they stopped?"

"Because they didn't do it by force," Wiggs explains. "Each country asked to join Tanzania. The people of those countries had to take a special vote, to make sure most of the population wanted to join. The voting in several of the countries went against joining, and so those countries didn't become a part of Tanzania."

"Countries used to be proud of their independence, though," I point out, intending to press the matter until I understand. "Why would they vote to let another country take them over?"

"The world was in a mess," Wiggs explains, pushing against the couch so that he can sit up straighter. "Economies had collapsed. Basically, things were spiraling out of control. Except in Tanzania. Tanzania had plenty of food. Their economy was booming. The unemployment rate was almost nonexistent. Other countries saw this and joined Tanzania as a way of saving their people."

"So they could either let another country take over, or watch their population starve to death and wipe each other out in civil wars?" I ask, beginning to understand.

"It's not as simple as that," Wiggs says, "but that's the general idea."

Nodding, I pause my hairstyling to scratch my nose and scope out the landscape. Most of the goatee is untangled. Soon I'll be able to start the actual trimming. Just as I reach over to tackle the last few inches of the goatee, Rafiki springs from my pocket and darts down my arm.

"If you would just – eek!" Wiggs screeches, jumping several inches. The look on his face is hilarious. "A mouse!"

"This is Rafiki," I explain, corralling the little guy and trying to hold in my laughter. "He's not a mouse. I picked him up on the storm planet." I can't contain my laughter any longer. It bubbles out of me like a warm spring. "You're lucky I haven't gotten to the shears yet. You probably would have jabbed yourself when you jumped… then you would have been in some *real* pain."

I move around the couch and hold Rafiki up for inspection. "See? Not a mouse."

"Look at his big eyes," Wiggs says. "He is a cute little guy. Does the captain know about him?"

"No, and it's going to stay that way," I respond firmly.

"Of course," Wiggs says. "My lips are sealed. What does he eat?"

"So far I've been feeding him leaves and berries," I say. Placing Rafiki on top of the game console so he can survey the room, I return to my hairstyling duties. "I think he might also eat meat, though, judging by his teeth."

"That's very possible," Wiggs says. "I have a hunk I'm preparing for my spaghetti sauce. When you're done torturing me, perhaps we can see what he thinks of it."

It takes a long time to hack my way through the jungle of Wiggs's hair. Even so, I have to surrender long before I feel I'm done. The goatee is looking pretty good – it's nearly untangled, and I've trimmed about four inches off its length. His hair is another matter; I've barely made a dent in the tangles. Right now, though, my hands are cramping badly, and I think the shears need to spend some time with a whetstone before I tackle the mess again.

"I've done what I can for today," I say, scooping Rafiki up and plopping him down on my shoulder. "Give my hands a few days to recover, and I'll work on it some more."

"What have you done?" Wiggs asks, eyeing me suspiciously. "Is one side of my hair really long and the other short?"

"No, nothing like that," I say, laughing. "It looks fine. I just want to do a bit more trimming."

Wiggs scowls. "You sure I'm not going to be the laughing-stock of the *Aurora*?"

"I promise you won't be." After all, if nobody has picked up on Dad's disastrous hairdo, I doubt they'll notice anything wrong with Wiggs. They probably won't even be able to tell he's had a trim. "What about that meat?" I ask.

"I'll get it. Just give me a sec," Wiggs says, heaving himself to his feet. The big guy crosses the room, humming. He pulls a flank of meat from a cupboard, a knife from the counter, and slices off a chunk. Returning to the couch, he holds the meat up for Rafiki to inspect.

The little guy's nose twitches. I feel Rafiki tense for a moment, and then he snatches at the meat, almost tumbling off my shoulder in his eagerness to grab the morsel. His claws dig into my skin, making me yelp.

"Easy, there," I say, helping him to steady himself. He's already tearing into the chunk, ripping off mouthfuls and gobbling them down. The meat is gone in seconds.

"Wow," I say, gazing at him in wonder. "He's never that enthusiastic about eating greens."

"It looks like these guys are omnivores, but with a decided preference for meat," Wiggs agrees dryly. "Here, I'll get him a bit more."

I watch Rafiki gnaw down several more small chunks like a buzz saw set on high gear, and wonder if I will ever be able to convince him to eat his veggies again.

———

"Quiet, Rafiki," I say, as I cautiously peer around the corner. Sharden almost spotted me when he exited the elevator. I dashed back around the wishbone junction just in time. Now I'm at the end of the portside corridor, waiting to see whether he's going to the bridge, or to his quarters. If he passes by the bridge, I'll have a hard time ducking into the lounge before I'm spotted. Rafiki seems to sense my excitement. The little guy is wriggling and moaning, trying to get a better view from my shirt pocket.

Here he comes! I glue myself to the wall and peer carefully around the edge. He's coming this way!

I sprint to the lounge. The door barely opens in time. I take a quick step into the room, hit something, hear a loud grunt, and go spinning to the floor. My Stratagem devices go flying out of my hands. Rafiki tries to creep out. I hastily stuff him farther down into his hiding spot, and then scramble to retrieve my devices.

"Ow! Why are you charging through doors like that?"

I look up from the deck and see that it's Waph. "I'm sorry," I say. "I was —"

"What's going on in here?" Sharden demands. He can smell trouble a mile away. And of course he has to stick his nose where it doesn't belong.

"Nothing, just an accident," I say quickly, trying to hold my Stratagem devices out of view.

"What are you doing on the floor, then?" Sharden asks sharply. "It doesn't look like nothing to me."

"We just bumped into each other, that's all," Waph intervenes. "Come, I'll help you with the calibrations on the temporagraph." Waph places his hand on Sharden's shoulder and steers him toward the bridge. Sharden takes one last look at me, his lip curls in a sneer, and then he heads off with Waph.

Whew. That was close!

I wait, my heart hammering, for a count of twenty. The door swishes open, and I look out. The corridor is clear. Should I continue on, or should I abort the mission? A vibrating moan from Rafiki seems to urge me on. Taking a deep breath, I trot toward the wishbone junction.

"All clear," I whisper to Rafiki, after snatching a glimpse of the starboard corridor. "Let's go."

The elevator is at the level of the holds. Of course. I wait tensely as it rises. A swish from the wishbone junction tells me the bridge hatch has opened. Come on, hurry up!

The elevator doors slide apart and I dash in, clearing the doorway before the doors are fully open. I wait, my heart beating rapidly, as they remain open. Footsteps approach. Who is it? Will they see me?

Finally, the doors whoosh together and the lift descends. That was too close!

When I reach the holds, I quickly check each one. There's nobody around. It's time to set up my devices!

"These are stun balls," I explain to Rafiki. "They give you a jolt and stiffen your suit for two full minutes. You can't move at all. Your opponent can attack you at his leisure and knock you out of the game. Today, though, they're going to be our targets."

I set each one carefully at a different spot in the hold. Even though I know where they're at, the three targets won't be easy to hit.

"This is a cloak," I say, once the stun balls are in place. "We're going to wrap ourselves in it to protect us from Howlers and Gushers." I drape the cloak over my shoulders and link the fastener.

"This little device is important," I tell Rafiki, holding up a small disc. "It dampens sound, making it harder for opponents to hear you." I activate the disc and set it in a pocket of my shorts.

"Now it's time for stealth mode. You'll have to ride up here." I carefully remove Rafiki from my pocket and place him on my shoulder. Once he has his balance, I lower my body slowly to the deck until I'm lying flat on my stomach. "Here, you're going to have to move a bit," I whisper, giggling as Rafiki's fur tickles my ear. I move him several inches away from my neck.

"Time to hunt," I say, easing the crossbow over a bit so it won't bother me when I snake forward. "Remember, you have to help me find the stun balls."

We creep along behind a row of crates. There's a gap where a crate has been removed. I cautiously peek around the edge of a wooden shipping container. Rafiki snuffles and makes a melodic whine.

"Did you spot something?" I ask, twisting my neck around so I can see the little guy out of the corner of my eye. His large, solemn eyes lock onto mine. He shakes his head; his mouth opens, exposing rows of tiny teeth as he moans. "Over in that direction? Okay."

I slip into the gap between crates. My eyes catch a glint. "You're right! I see it too," I whisper. Moving very slowly, I ease the crossbow around so that the stock is snug against my right shoulder. It's already loaded with the first quarrel. Taking a bead on the stun ball, I draw in a slow breath and hold it. I have the target centered in my sights. I squeeze the trigger.

With a barely audible thunk, the bolt is away. It makes very little sound as it passes through the air. A split second later, it thuds against the side of a crate and bounces to the floor. "That was a lousy shot," I grumble to Rafiki, feeling disappointment settling in my stomach. I missed by half a foot!

"You have to reload very slowly and quietly, otherwise you'll soon become a target," I explain to Rafiki. "It's awkward, but necessary."

It takes me almost a full minute to fit a fresh quarrel onto the crossbow. I line up my shot and fire.

"Got it!" I whisper proudly to Rafiki. "Though in a real game, I probably wouldn't have gotten a second shot. It's important to hit your target on the first attempt."

I slither behind a new row of shipping containers into a tall, narrow alley. It takes several minutes to reach the end. Rafiki gives an excited whine. There is a sudden pain in my ear. Rafiki nipped me! It doesn't really hurt – it surprises me more than anything. I look at him out of the corner of my eye. His eyes are focused on something up ahead. He is still whining. His little body is shaking.

"You see another one?" I whisper, deciding to ignore the nip. I don't even have to look fully around the corner for confirmation – I can see the stun ball reflected in the smooth bulkhead. "You have sharp eyes!

"This is going to be tricky. I have to poke my nose too far from cover. Hopefully he won't be looking this way!"

I fit another bolt into the crossbow, slide past the end of the crate, and take aim. "Bam! Another hit, Rafiki!" I exclaim, rising to my feet. "And that's how it's done. What did you think of your first game of Stratagem?" Rafiki gives a snort, and then a series of clicks. "Yeah, I agree. It *would* be more fun with real opponents. Maybe someday you'll get to see an actual game. For now, though, we'd better collect our gear and clear out before we're discovered."

I grab everything. Just as I'm about to exit the hold, the elevator doors slide open. I jump back out of sight and wait, muscles tense, as I listen to the sound of footsteps. There are at least two sets. They seem to be coming this way! My eyes dart around, searching for a better hiding spot. The footsteps are right outside the hold…

There. Someone has pulled a couple of crates out from the wall and shifted them to one side in order to gain access to a control panel. There is now a small gap between them and the neighboring crates. I doubt I can fit behind them, but it's the only cover I can find.

I dash over and squeeze into the gap. Did I make it in time?

"Just a moment," I hear Sharden mutter. Of all the rotten luck, it has to be him. One set of footsteps approaches my hiding spot. He must have caught a glimpse of me! My heart pounds painfully in my chest. What am I going to say when he drags me out of hiding?

A moment later I hear a whirring noise, which quickly builds to a rattling hum. I wait tensely for him to pounce. After several thudding heartbeats, I decide that he hasn't spotted me after all. He just came over to start up… whatever it is he started up. I puzzle over the sound. What kind of machinery would Sharden need to use down here?

"Now we can talk," he says above the hum. Oh, so that's what this is about. He's started the machinery to create noise. He doesn't want his conversation to be overheard. Which means he must be up to something.

"What's this about?" a voice growls. It's Marcum. His voice comes from barely a yard away. I try to make myself even smaller.

"The captain's lost it," Sharden says, his voice barely audible above the rumble of machinery. "He's having a nervous breakdown. He isn't fit to command."

"I see no evidence of that," Marcum says guardedly.

"He won't let me review the navigational data to make sure we've truly reversed course. He won't let Johnson calculate possible alternate courses. And…" Sharden pauses a moment, creating a sense of anticipation for what he will say next. "The captain broke down in my cabin, blathering about how we're lost and we'll never find our way back. He was on the verge of tears."

I can't imagine this. The captain, always brimming with confidence and bluster, breaking down? Almost crying? It can't be true.

"The captain's fine," Marcum says. Evidently he can't believe it either. "He's in command, and that won't change."

Sharden wants the captain removed from command. I don't particularly like the captain. But to take away his command? That's a little extreme. I really don't see how that would do us any good. I'm glad Marcum is setting him right. He isn't having anything to do with this.

"How long have we got?" Sharden asks. This swift change in topic throws me. What is he talking about?

Marcum isn't confused, though. This must be something they've discussed before, because he answers promptly. "Three, maybe four more weeks, depending on how we use the engines."

Iridium. That's what this new topic is. Which means we have three or four more weeks to find a planet, locate iridium, mine it, and purify it. My heart drops at the thought. It could be months, or even longer, before we find another planet.

"Three weeks. We don't have time to bumble around, hoping we magically hit the right spot. We have to do this scientifically!"

"The captain is in command," Marcum repeats. Although this time, it seems there's a hint of uncertainty in his voice.

"Perhaps," Sharden says. For several seconds the only sound I hear is the rattle of the engine. With a sudden cough, the hum winds down and then cuts off completely. Once the ringing in my ears fades, I hear the sound of breathing nearby. I tense up, barely daring to breathe myself. Rafiki seems to understand the need for absolute silence. He doesn't let out a peep.

Finally, footsteps ring against the deck, heading for the hatch. The lift doors swish open, and then swish closed again. I still can't relax. There was only one set of footsteps leaving. One of them could still be here.

I wait in silence, ears pricked for any hint of sound. There is the whisper of the ventilation system, the occasional click, ping, or hum of distant machinery – normal sounds in any interstellar ship – but no sign of any person nearby. Marcum must have left while the machine was still operating; the noise would have easily drowned out his footsteps. Can I risk a peek? If Sharden finds out I've heard the conversation, I will be in deep trouble.

I wait another couple of minutes, calling on my half-forgotten Stratagem skills of patience and stealth. Finally, I slowly ease my right eye around the edge of the top crate. No one there. Continuing to listen for any sign of danger, I lean out a bit farther. Still no sign of life.

Taking a breath, gulping down my fear, I step forward and carefully scan the bay around me. There's no one in sight. Still, a row of stacked crates blocks my view to the left. There's a chance one of them went back there. I slowly emerge from my spot, stretch my legs, and tiptoe over to the row of crates. Pause to listen. Nothing. Peek around the corner. The area is clear. A bit of my tension drains away. But I can't relax completely. One of them might come back before I can get out of here.

After checking the area outside the hold, I dash to the elevator, stuffing Rafiki back into my pocket on the way. There's no one in the starboard corridor when the lift opens. I head toward my room at a fast clip, relieved that I have escaped undetected.

Suddenly, a voice from the bridge brings me to a halt.

"I don't know what it is," Johnson says.

"Do you think it's dangerous?" the captain asks.

"There's no way of knowing yet," Johnson replies.

What's happening? What are they talking about? I turn toward the bridge, anxious to see what the fuss is about.

My Stratagem devices! I don't want the captain to see them. He might get suspicious.

I hurry to my cabin, dump the devices on my bed, and scurry back to the bridge. The object they are looking at is immediately obvious: there is a dark smudge in the rainbow of colors. A place devoid of light.

"Is that a black hole?" I ask. The possibility is interesting, but I definitely don't want to find out the hard way.

"We're not sure what it is," says Johnson. "It would be wise to keep our distance, though."

"We will," the captain promises. "Hold this course for five more light-minutes, and then bring us to full stop." I watch him out of the corner of my eye. Is Sharden right? Has the captain snapped?

I don't see any evidence of this. The captain's chest puffs out as always, his back is straight, his eyes still attack everything they see. He doesn't look broken at all.

The *Aurora* creeps closer. One hour ticks by. A second hour crawls calmly past. Eventually, the dark blotch takes on a more definitive shape – it looks like a globe of black smoke. The edges are blurred; it doesn't seem like a black hole, but what could it be?

"I've set an orbit, Captain," Johnson says.

The captain looks thoughtful for a moment. "We need information. Kartak, prepare and launch a pod. Set a simple trajectory, closest approach thirty miles, with a return to our orbital path for pickup."

"That's an awfully close pass," Kartak says.

"With the sensors the way they are, we have to if we're to get any data," the captain points out immediately. The captain is making quick decisions. He wouldn't be able to do this if he has cracked. Sharden is wrong. What if he still tries to get the captain booted from his position? Being in this weird space is bad enough. If the adults start fighting amongst themselves, our chances of getting home will grow even slimmer. The problem is, there's nothing I can do about it. I have to try to put Sharden's plan out of my mind.

"Very well, Captain," Kartak says, and heads for the lower deck.

It's almost twenty minutes before I see a pod streaking toward the dark mass. If that thing's a black hole, the pod will disappear, never to be seen again. If it's something else… the pod will hopefully give us a better idea of what it might be.

"We should be intercepting it in about one hundred twenty-five minutes," Kartak says, reentering the bridge. "I'm not sure how accurate the course is that I plotted, so we'll have to keep a sharp lookout."

"Very well," the captain replies. "Waph and Hollins, I want you as spotters in the lounge. Kartak, I want you and Sean spotting from the bridge. Let's get this pod found!"

The task reminds me of leaving the storm planet, and the days we spent scanning for the *Aurora*. At least we have an idea of when and where the pod will be. The problem is, it's much smaller than the *Aurora*. It'll be hard to spot. And if we miss it, the pod will fly right on by and disappear into the void between the stars, and we'll never see it again. I can't let that happen.

Almost three full minutes ahead of schedule, I spot something floating off to starboard. "There it is!" I announce, pointing toward the pod.

"Great!" the captain roars. "Kartak and Yates, go secure it. Let's find out what the devil that is out there."

We move as a group toward the turbolift. Kartak, Dad, Sharden, Johnson, and the captain ride down first.

I want to squeeze in with the second group, but with Wiggs taking up half the elevator, there isn't room. By the time I'm down, Kartak and Dad have just about finished suiting up. Rafiki pokes his head out to take in the activity. "Here, get back... oh, never mind," I say, deciding the captain will be too focused on the pod to notice.

Dad and Kartak enter the airlock, and the waiting begins.

The airlock cycles. I picture Kartak and Dad anchoring themselves with cables, opening the outer hatch, and gazing around to sight the pod. How long will that take? Then they will launch toward the pod and use maneuvering thrusters to correct their course. They should be reaching it right about now. Next comes the tricky task of grappling the pod and towing it back in. That will take a while. Right about now they should be settling the pod on the deck of the airlock, closing the outer hatch, and beginning decontamination.

The minutes tick by. My gaze is fixed on the airlock hatch, expecting it to open at any moment. Surely they should be done by now. What if their cables came loose, or an asteroid sliced through their tethers? What if the pod drifted out of range, or they can't spot it in the rainbow?

I realize I'm tapping my foot and force myself to stop. I take a couple of deep breaths. I have to relax. Everything is going to be fine. It just takes longer to corral the pod than I anticipate. Any moment now the lock hatch will open...

Another five minutes pass. Ten. At fifteen minutes I'm really starting to worry. I turn and whisper to Wiggs. "Do you think something's happened?"

"Why don't you ask them?" Wiggs says, a little smirk on his face.

"What do you mean?" I ask. Turning back to the airlock hatch, my confusion clears. The hatch opened while I was turned away. Kartak and Dad are herding the pod through on a hovercart.

"Yes, they made it!" I whisper to Rafiki.

———

It turns out the dark blob is a planet – at least, that's our assumption. It has an atmosphere. Unless the black holes in this weird region of space have atmospheres, it's a safe bet we're looking at a planet.

"Are we sending an exploration team?" Roberts asks, sitting up a little in his bed. I'm glad he has recovered so well. Those strong-jaw wounds were nasty. He takes another bite of soup as he awaits my response.

"We still need iridium since we didn't find any on the storm planet," I reply. "A team is due to leave tomorrow after breakfast."

Roberts' left eye starts to wander as he reflects on my news. "I think I'll sit this one out," he says, before taking another slurp of soup. A stream of broth dribbles off his chin. "I've had enough of alien planets for the moment."

"I doubt the captain expects you to go on a landing party," I reassure him. "You'll be in sickbay at least a few more days. We might be finished by then."

"And a good thing, too," he says. "Rita must be getting mighty anxious by now. I say we cut this trip short and return home."

Evidently, he's forgotten that we haven't found a way back yet. I decide to leave him his delusion. "I had better get going. I promised Wiggs I would finish his haircut. See you around!"

"Be careful going down there," Roberts says as I rise to leave. "You don't want to end up like me."

The thought makes me shudder. I know he's talking about the wounds from the strong-jaws, but when he says this, I immediately think of his goofy face and wandering mind. I definitely don't want to end up like him. "I doubt I'll be going to the planet," I reply, happy that he can't read my thoughts. "But if I do, you can be sure I'll be very careful."

CHAPTER 15

The Key

"Roberts is dead."

The words stun me. It hardly seems possible. I was speaking with him just yesterday. His fever was gone. Most of his scabs had disappeared, replaced by smooth new skin. He was telling me how he only had one more day in bed, and then he would be back on his feet.

Today he's dead. How can that be possible? The thought completely numbs my mind.

"The first trip down will be postponed," the captain says. "Waph, I want you to arrange the funeral."

"How did it happen?" I ask, finding my voice at last.

"Some kind of infection," Kartak says. "We seemed to have it beaten, but it must have gone dormant for a while. When it became active again, it attacked quickly and savagely. It spread throughout his body within a couple of hours."

"Funeral will be at 1800," the captain says. "We will convene at the airlock at that time."

I leave sickbay in a daze. I've never truly realized how fragile life can be. One minute you're relaxing in bed, joking and laughing. The next minute… I don't want to complete the thought.

<hr>

The funeral is a somber affair. Waph reads a passage from an old naval memorial service. We are quiet for a few minutes. Everyone is completely still. There is no shifting of feet or movement of fingers. The captain says a final blessing. The outer airlock door opens. A small puff of air in the lock creates a push to get Roberts' body moving. It glides slowly and silently into the vastness of space, where it will orbit this black planet until the world ends.

Impossibly, Rafiki seems affected by Roberts' death. He becomes very quiet, and hardly moves at all. I know that dogs can often pick up on moods. Is Rafiki reading my emotions? Or could he be sick? This thought is depressing. I would have no idea how to cure him. I'm so anxious about Rafiki, I don't even go to see the first landing party off.

"What's wrong?" I ask, cuddling Rafiki in my arms – he no longer fits in my pocket. He's about the size of a human baby. At this rate, I won't be able to keep him hidden much longer.

Rafiki simply stares at me with his liquid eyes. I pull a fist-size hunk of meat from my pocket. He perks up at once, tearing into the meat and swallowing large chunks. "Hey, careful!" I say. "I don't want you to choke."

After the last bite is swallowed, Rafiki nuzzles my hand, then settles back down. He's soon asleep. I lower him gently to my bunk and head out the door.

"Computer, how long has the landing party been gone?" I ask as I walk to the bridge.

"The lander launched fourteen minutes twelve point nine seconds ago," the computer replies.

My eyes scan the bridge and note that Kartak, Hollins, and Waph are gone. That's who's on the landing party. Everyone else is sitting facing the viewport. Conversations are short and clipped, tension evident in the voices. I find an empty chair and sit down.

I can't focus. My thoughts cycle between Rafiki's peculiar mood, and what the landing party is doing. Why is the planet so dark? What kind of surface does it have?

"The landing party has returned," the computer says, almost four hours later. I was just about to grab a snack. That will have to wait. We rush to the landing bay.

"Computer, how much longer for the decontamination cycle to finish?" I hear the captain ask as I step from the elevator.

"There are seventeen minutes left in the cycle," the computer replies.

Seventeen minutes. That's plenty of time to check on Rafiki and grab a snack. I step back into the lift and head for my cabin.

Rafiki is still snoozing when I arrive. This isn't like him. He must be sick. What can I possibly do about it?

After thinking about the problem for a while, I decide the best thing to do is let him rest, and make sure he drinks lots of water. That's what Mom was always reminding me of when I was sick.

I gently stroke Rafiki's fur with my finger, being careful not to wake him. His body vibrates with each deep breath he takes. "You need to get better soon," I whisper.

Not sure how much time has passed, I quickly grab a couple of carrots as I pass hydroponics, and set out for the elevator at a jog. I don't want to miss anything about the planet!

It takes a few more minutes for the decontamination cycle to end. There is a lot of shifting of feet and tense glances as we wait impatiently for the landing party to emerge. Soon the landing bay hatch opens. Kartak steps out. He shakes his head.

"It's like nothing I've ever seen," he says, combing his hand through his hair. "It's completely dark down there. We couldn't see anything. The lander's spotlights didn't work at all. I just checked them, and they're working fine now. I don't know what happened. I was almost afraid to land, because I couldn't tell what I was landing on. But we set down okay."

"It was eerie," Hollins says, coming up beside Kartak. "Complete darkness everywhere. Our helmet lights didn't work either. We didn't venture far from the ship; simply collected a couple of rock samples and came straight back up."

"How about the lander?" I ask, wondering what could be causing the darkness.

"What about it?" Kartak grunts.

"Were the lights inside the lander working?" I ask, trying to visualize the situation.

"Yep," Kartak replies. "The interior lighting and all the instrument lights worked just fine. It was only the lights outside the lander that didn't work."

"And the airlock," Hollins adds.

"Yeah, that was crazy as well," says Kartak. "Going out, we had light in the airlock. As soon as the exterior hatch opened, the lights went out. It was pitch black inside the airlock when we got back in. About half-way through the decontamination cycle, the lights came back on."

This gets me thinking. Could something be draining the power to the lights? No, that doesn't make sense. If the energy was drained, how would the airlock lights suddenly get power back in the middle of a cycle? Also, it didn't affect any of the other systems in the suits or the lander, including the interior lights.

"Microbes," Sharden mutters.

"What?" the captain asks sharply.

"Microscopic organisms that have evolved to absorb light," Sharden says. "They are killed during the decontamination process."

"It's as good a theory as any," Kartak says, nodding thoughtfully.

"Did you try ultraviolet lamps?" Wiggs asks.

"We didn't have any with us," Hollins replies promptly.

"I doubt it would make any difference," adds Waph. "Remember, the light in this region doesn't behave like the light we're used to."

"Still, it's worth a try," the captain says. "The next landing party will carry ultraviolet and infrared lamps. Kartak, I want you, Hollins, and Yates on the next away team. You will leave at 0700 tomorrow. See if you can locate an iridium deposit. We must get some soon!"

"Yes sir," Kartak replies.

The second team has no luck with the infrared or ultraviolet lamps. No light source works on the planet. The teams are unable to search for iridium because of this – they have no way of reading the scanner. How can we locate iridium if we can't see?

Somehow, the total darkness of the planet sounds familiar. But I can't figure out why. I sit on my bunk petting Rafiki as I ponder the problem. He's dozing again. He has slept most of the past three days. I'm beginning to wonder if it has something to do with the animals hibernating on the storm planet. Is there something that makes him think it's time for hibernation? There aren't any storms aboard the *Aurora*. I just don't know what would trigger his instincts.

A third exploration team returns from the planet. One look at Kartak's face tells me they didn't have any luck.

"The welders, plasma torches, and arc lamps didn't give out any light, either," he confirms as he pulls his suit off. "Neither did the refraction lens – although I thought that was a great idea, Sean." This makes me proud. I thought that trying to refract the light of a lamp using a lens might get us somewhere. Apparently, I was wrong. "I think we should push on," Kartak concludes.

This comment is met with silence. I think back to the conversation I overheard in the hold. We have three or four weeks of iridium left. We can't possibly find another planet before then. Surely Marcus knows this. Will he speak up? I don't want to say anything. If I mention the three or four weeks, Marcus will demand to know how I found out.

"We'll give it a little more time," the captain says, relieving the pressure in my chest. We're staying. We still have a chance. "Perhaps we can rig the scanner so that we can find iridium without being able to see. Kartak, I want you and Marcum to work on the problem."

"Yes sir," Marcum replies. Kartak just nods.

Thinking about our situation is nerve-racking. I need something to occupy my mind. Spotting Waph offloading rock and soil samples from the dark planet, I jog over.

"I can help you with that," I offer, grabbing one of the containers.

"Thanks, Sean. It would be good to have your eyes and mind," Waph replies. "We'll bring these to Lab C."

I follow him to a small compartment toward the rear of the ship on the starboard side. A lot of the scanners don't work in the rainbow light, so most of our observations are done by sight, smell, and touch.

"What sample are we on?" I ask, as I set down my load.

"Twenty-eight rock and soil samples have been categorized," the computer replies. "The next sample will be number twenty-nine."

"Sample twenty-nine," I confirm, picking up a golf ball-sized rock. I rub my fingers along the surface. "It feels a bit spongy," I say. "Definitely porous, with a tiny bit of give when I push down with my thumb. It smells a bit like clay." I hand the sample over to Waph. "Your turn."

He notes his observations, and then we begin all over again with sample thirty. It's a long, tedious process. Just as I'm beginning to think the exploration team brought back a bottomless sample container, I feel around and find one final sample. This one feels like a gemstone – hard and smooth. It doesn't have any smell that I can detect.

"Well, that's it," Waph says, after finishing his analysis. He rubs his eyes and yawns. "I'm guessing it's about supper time. Let's go see what Wiggs has for us tonight."

My stomach gives a rumble of agreement. When we arrive, we find that everyone else has started without us. Waph and I take our seats and quickly dish up plates of rice from a storage hold and meat from the storm planet. We've been eating pretty much the same food for the past couple of weeks, but I'm too hungry to care. I shovel large spoonfuls into my mouth.

"Any luck with adapting the scanner?" Waph asks as he digs in.

"Not yet," Kartak replies. "There has to be a way to use sound pulses, but we can't think of exactly how to make it work."

"How about other light sources we haven't thought of?" Hollins asks.

"According to the computer, we've tried everything we have on board," Marcum growls. "We can't count on being able to see."

Thinking about the dark planet, I am once again struck by the thought that it's somehow familiar. I have seen something similar. The answer is right there, at the edge of my brain. I try concentrating, but that seems to make the answer vanish. It's frustrating. Why can't I remember?

I shrug and return to my food. The answer will probably hit me in the middle of the night.

I'm really worried about Rafiki now. Day and night he sleeps curled up at the foot of my bed. He only stirs long enough to chomp down two meals each day. And his appetite is growing. The captain is getting suspicious about how quickly the meat is being consumed. Any day now, the captain is sure to come investigate my cabin and find the little guy.

Also, this morning Rafiki snapped at me. If I hadn't jumped back to the other side of the cabin, he may have kept chewing. At the time there was a red stripe on my arm, and I immediately thought of Roberts. Fortunately, his teeth didn't sink in. The red line is gone; the skin isn't broken. I should be safe.

It's his supper time. I stand a couple of yards back and toss him the last of the leaves. He attacks them in a frenzy, as if he hasn't eaten in a week. I add several hunks of meat and a lump of cheese. They are gone in seconds. He sniffs around for any stray morsel he may have missed, and then settles to the deck.

Perhaps Stratagem will liven him up. I don't know how I can get him to the hold unseen. But if it helps perk him up, I'm willing to take the risk.

I want to try some devices I haven't used in a long time. The robots and Howler would make too much noise. I look under the bunk. A rainbow-colored glint catches my eye, sending a jolt through my body. That's it! That's what the dark planet reminds me of!

I grab the device and dash out the door, wondering if this could be the key to finding the iridium.

CHAPTER 16

Deep Darkness

Thoughts whirl through my mind as I hurry to the bridge. Images of Stratagem games I've played. Memories of the first time the sudden darkness descended upon me: I had lost half my points to a Marauder attack. I was huddled behind the shield casing for an immense B-130 rocket engine. The sun was hot, oppressive, and then suddenly… gone. Replaced by utter blackness. It took me a few seconds to work out what had happened. By the time I recovered from the shock, it was too late. A robotic Otter finished me off. That was the last time I lost at Stratagem.

When I first set eyes on the Occluder in my cabin, I was certain it was the solution to our problem. On Earth, the Occluder shuts out light. Might it do the opposite here? It's a wild theory, but nothing else has worked. I figure it's worth a try.

However, the more I think about it, the more foolish it sounds. Why would this little device allow us to see on the dark planet? What help could it possibly give? Do I really want to suggest it to the scientists? I halt outside the bridge hatch, rooted in place, horrified that I have been about to make such a stupid suggestion to the adults.

But no. I had my doubts about the Daystrum Rings. That had been worth trying. This might be, too. It may not work, but that doesn't make it a bad idea.

Summoning all of my courage, I open the hatch and step onto the bridge. Five people are present: the captain, Johnson, Wiggs, Waph, and Sharden. The sight of the grouchy old man makes me hesitate a moment.

"I have an idea," I say, before I lose my nerve.

The captain's eyes attack me. I feel myself shrink back. I'm losing my nerve again…

"What's this about?" he demands. "What idea?"

"This is a Stratagem device called an Occluder," I say. Holding it out where the adults can see it, I fight down a ripple of unease that flutters in my stomach.

"You've come here to bother us with games?" Sharden says with a sneer.

I keep my eyes on the captain and try to block Sharden from my mind. "It creates a field of darkness around an opponent. I thought perhaps it might do the opposite here," I conclude, my voice trailing off. Saying it makes the idea sound even more ridiculous. My eyes drop to the floor. I can't bear to look at anyone. What must they be thinking? "Anyway, it's just a thought," I mumble. I have to get out of here, I have to hide from this humiliation –

"And a good one," Wiggs says.

"Good?" Sharden retorts sarcastically. "It's a waste of time. We need to focus on altering the scanner to an audio mode."

The captain nods in agreement. "That's our priority," he says.

"Sean's idea is the best one we've had," Johnson says.

I look up. His face looks cautiously eager.

"Fixing the scanner so we can hear it is the best idea," Sharden insists.

The argument goes back and forth. Wiggs and Johnson are in favor of trying the Occluder. Sharden and the captain keep shooting the idea down. My opinion sinks and soars with each point given.

Eventually, Johnson lets out a breath in exasperation. "Why are we arguing about this? Let's just try it and see what happens!"

The bridge falls silent for a moment. I shift my feet, wondering what's going through the captain's mind.

"You're right, of course," he says at last. "Wiggs, fetch Kartak. I want the two of you ready to go in one hour!"

I scramble out the door, feeling hope rise in my chest. Perhaps we'll be able to find some iridium after all.

———

The wait seems endless. I pace outside the landing bay hatch – I can't bear to leave it, even for a moment. I realize I'm biting my fingernails. Forcing my hands into my pockets, I think back to my instructions to Kartak. Was I clear on how to operate the wrist monitor and Occluder? I should be down there. I'm the one who knows how to operate the devices.

A noise makes me jerk my head around. It's the elevator door. The captain strides out, followed by Johnson, Sharden, and Dad. The lander must be ready to dock.

A few minutes later, the computer confirms it. "Shuttle has landed. All systems appear normal."

They are back, but I still have to wait for the decontamination cycle to finish. Scattered conversations break out among the adults. I resume my pacing.

"Decontamination complete," the computer states after another eternity.

The hatch door opens slowly. Kartak and Wiggs appear, looking haggard. It didn't work. Our last chance to find iridium is gone. I feel as if molten lead has been poured into my body.

"There's good news, and there's bad news," Kartak rasps, his voice sounding as tired as his body looks. "The good news is, the Occluder works. We were able to see within two yards around us." This should make me feel better. My idea has worked. However, the look on Kartak's face steals all the excitement away. I already know what the bad news is going to be. They didn't find any iridium.

I'm concentrating on my thoughts, and almost miss Kartak's next statement. "The bad news is, neither of us could read the scanner. The image was too poor."

A seed of hope and excitement sprouts inside me. There's still a chance! "Let me try," I say eagerly.

"It's too dangerous!" Dad says immediately.

"Running out of iridium would be too dangerous," I point out. "We need to be able to read the scanner. I have the best eyes. Let me try!"

The captain's brow furrows. He's doing some heavy thinking.

"Let me take Sean down right away," Kartak says. "If there is iridium down there, it may take time to locate it."

I can see an instant change on the captain's face. He nods. "Do it," he orders.

Dad opens his mouth to argue, then closes it again. He knows just as well as anybody how crucial the success of this mission is. We can't afford to play it safe. Sighing, Dad comes up and puts a hand on my shoulder. "I know you can do this. Be safe."

"I will," I promise him. He gives my shoulder a squeeze, and then releases it. Kartak is almost to the lander. I'm about to follow when I suddenly think of Rafiki. I might be gone a while. Panicked, I turn toward the elevator. "I'll be back in a moment!"

"What! Where are you going?" the captain thunders behind me. I ignore him.

As soon as the elevator doors open on the upper level, I rush to the kitchen, grab several chunks of meat, and hurry to my cabin. Rafiki is curled up on my bed.

"I'll be back soon," I say, kissing the soft fur of his head. "Get healthy."

I don't want to leave him when he isn't feeling well, but this mission is of the utmost importance. I must go.

Taking one last look at him, I zip back to the elevator. Once down, I grab my suit and head for the landing bay. There's Wiggs. To my relief, he's standing slightly apart from the rest of the adults. I hurry over and whisper, "Take care of the little guy," into his ear. Without waiting for a response – I'm certain he understands – I jog to the lander, feeling a mixture of giddiness and apprehension. Once again, the fate of the *Aurora* is on my shoulders. I can't fail!

Acceleration pushes me back in my seat as the lander slips from the hold. Soon we are diving toward the absolute darkness. It isn't like the holos I've seen of Earth's night side – those glitter with brilliant jewels and webs of light. This isn't the black of night. As far as I can tell, the planet's star is shining from about thirty degrees off our port side; the globe should be bathed in its rainbow-colored light. No, this is a different sort of blackness, from an unknown source. I feel my skin tingle at the thought. I'm not afraid of the dark. This dark, however, might hold dangers I know nothing about.

Soon the blackness envelopes us. I can't see anything through the viewport in any direction. My muscles tense. A sudden thought occurs to me.

"How will you land if you can't see the planet?" I know Kartak has brought the lander down safely on several other missions. How did he do it?

"Have you ever heard of echolocation?" he asks.

The word sounds familiar, but I can't place it. "I think so."

"It's what bats use to see in the dark," he explains.

"That's right! I remember reading about it in school," I say, recalling my excitement at learning of the bat's ability. For the next several days I was convinced that I could copy them, if I only concentrated hard enough.

"The lander has a system that works in a similar way," Kartak says. "It emits sound, and uses the echo to map the terrain. It's very useful on planets like Bolterrus, where the atmospheric conditions often scramble a ship's sensors."

"And dark planets," I add with a grin.

"Yes, and dark planets," Kartak agrees. "We should be landing in about thirty minutes."

I gaze at the blackness outside the viewport, darker than night. What could cause this? Why don't the lander's running lights work?

We hit turbulence, and I grip the armrests of my seat. What if there's a tree in our path that the lander can't detect? Okay, maybe not a tree, a tree couldn't live in this darkness, but some other kind of tall object. Or what if we smash into some kind of flying creature? Or what if this turbulence is the start of a storm, like on the ring planet? We would be stuck in the shuttle, surrounded by darkness and no way of getting more air…

I'm gripping the seat so tightly my hands are starting to cramp. I let go and take a deep breath. I have to calm down. We aren't going to crash, and we aren't going to get stranded in a storm. We're going to collect our iridium and get back to Rafiki, Dad, and the others.

The lander suddenly shakes and I'm thrown against my harness. Again I grab the armrests, preparing for the coming disaster…

"Well, it wasn't my smoothest of landings, but it wasn't my worst one, either," Kartak comments.

"What? You mean we're on the ground?" I ask, certain there has to be some other explanation for the huge jolt.

"We're down, and systems are going to standby," Kartak confirms, his fingers dancing over the controls. "According to the ship's sensors, there is a strong possibility of iridium nearby. Are you ready for this?"

Am I ready? I will be going out into the darkness alone, facing unknown dangers. I will only be able to see two yards around me. I will be connected to the lander by a lifeline, supplying me with air. The lifeline is strong, but what if it snaps? I would still have the reserve tank, so I wouldn't be without air. But in this total darkness, I could wander around within a few feet of the lander and never find it. Am I ready? Do I really have an option? I have to get going before my dread completely overwhelms me.

I pluck the Occluder from a pocket of my suit and grasp it firmly in my hand, wishing I didn't have the thick gloves on. The smooth sides of the familiar device could help steady my nerves. "As ready as I'll ever be," I say, hoping my voice doesn't quaver too much.

Kartak seems to understand how I feel. "Right," he says, quickly retrieving the scanner and a repeater from a locker at the rear of the cockpit. "Here's this," he says, handing me the scanner. He also loads me up with a sonic drill and a backpack which is sturdy but comfortable to wear. "Now let's get you hooked up."

He leads me to the airlock. There are four lifelines spooled up on the left wall, their ends held by clips near the deck. Kartak quickly and efficiently grabs one of the reinforced hoses and secures it to the connector of my suit. He then connects his own lifeline.

"Secure your helmet," he says, as he seals the inner hatch of the airlock. Kartak smiles. "Here we go." His nimble fingers quickly secure his helmet in place, he checks the seal on mine, and then hits the control to cycle the lock.

I don't activate the Occluder yet. I want to be able to find my way out of the lander without stumbling around like a fool. My muscles tremble as I wait for the lock to cycle. Can I do this?

A moment later, the outer hatch opens. Darkness rushes in much quicker than I anticipate. A complete, utter darkness that leaves me feeling absolutely helpless. I can't see a thing.

But I can certainly hear.

A chorus of mews, rumbles, warbles, screeches, snorts, bellows, growls, and plaintive cries filter through my helmet pickups. I fumble to activate the Occluder. Without gloves on I could do it easily. But now I can't feel the controller. My first attempt fails. Panic rises in my chest. Will something attack me before I flick it on? I desperately try again, and again, my finger flicking across the familiar surface of my wrist monitor. Come on, I have to get it activated…

Suddenly, I'm surrounded by a faint glow. A ghostly blue image flicks in and out of view. A wave of terror grips me. This is far worse than even the strong-jaws on the storm planet.

There I had Dad and Kartak to help protect me. Kartak is here, yes, but he can't see. There's no way he can help. I'm completely on my own. And I can't even spot danger until it's close enough to attack.

My knees lock up. I can't move. There has to be another way to get iridium!

A wave of dizziness hits. I take an involuntary step, stumble on the lip of the airlock, and lurch forward. My hands and knees hit the ground, sending a shock of pain through my wrists and forearms. I quickly scramble to regain my feet; I don't want an unseen predator to attack when I'm down.

Spotting the edge of the airlock, I grab on to steady myself. It takes a moment, but my head clears. And this helps me see the truth, crisply and clearly: I can't do this. Exiting the lander will mean certain death. I don't have what it takes to face the unknown terrors lurking out there. Somebody else will have to be the hero.

But that's the problem. No one else can read the scanner. None of the adults would be able to find the iridium.

I think back to Victoria: to the vacant lot, to the apartment, to my friends. If I'm ever going to get back there, we need to find iridium; *I* need to find iridium. Here. Now. On this planet. I have a job to do. The quicker I find the iridium, the sooner I can escape this nightmare.

I click on the scanner and hold the display close to my face. At first all I see is a blue blur. Soon it appears that numbers are forming in the blue blob. Is it just my mind playing tricks on me? I squint through my faceplate. There seems to be an arrow pointing to my left, and a set of numbers beneath it. I decide to trust that the scanner has detected iridium.

Turning in the direction of the arrow, trying to forget about the growls I hear and flashes I see at the edge of the Occluder's bubble, I set out into the deep darkness.

———

Each step takes me farther from the safety of the lander. The blue glow changes to green. My skin crawls at the howls and hisses picked up by my helmet's external microphones. I realize my heart is thumping like a piston of the ancient car my neighbor Drake raced proudly around the streets of Victoria. Again I stumble, and just catch myself before I fall. The ground is uneven, and the ghostly green light doesn't really illuminate the terrain.

The numbers on the scanner appear to be decreasing. I take this as a positive sign. I don't want to stop, but I also don't want to pass by an iridium deposit. I pause, and force my eyes to concentrate on the scanner. Does it say 8.09? That would mean I'm getting close.

Suddenly, something slams into me from behind, sending me lurching forward, back into a blue glow. My heart leaps into overdrive. This is it. A creature is attacking me!

My head snaps around. I catch a glimpse of something long and thin, like a tail. But then it's gone. Is the creature turning around for another pass? Will it bite me this time? Where will it attack from?

I get into a balanced stance and prepare myself, my muscles tense, my chest painfully tight. I pivot my head from side to side, scanning the blue bubble around me. Three seconds pass. Five. Nothing comes at me.

Where is it? I can't stand here forever!

After ten seconds, I decide the best thing to do is keep going. I long for light, even if it is rainbow colored. Anything that would help me see the things stalking around me. I know they're there. I can feel them, hear them, practically taste them. Will they coordinate an attack? My mind creates images of what the creatures must look like: all claws and teeth and stingers. My breaths come in short, jerky gasps. I must stop this!

Focus on the goal. That's what I must do.

Taking a deep breath to calm myself, I resume my trek. Fifteen steps on this uneven ground. That should be about eight yards. I stop and scrutinize the scanner again. The hazy image swims before my eyes. I blink a few times, trying to bring it into focus. It looks like it's at zero.

I grab the sonic drill and flick the power switch. As it activates, I press and hold a button to make the cut as narrow as possible. Until I'm more confident about where the iridium is, I want to make my digs as delicate as possible.

Pointing the drill at the ground about two feet from my boots, I squeeze the trigger. The drill vibrates slightly as it goes to work. I slowly walk in a circle, angling the drill to create a beveled edge.

Now I have to wait for it to cool.

Standing in my island of light, listening to the cacophony of sounds around me, I wonder what the land looks like. Is it a savanna? Or gully-cut hills? Is there any vegetation? I can't imagine any plants growing in this darkness, but perhaps they have another source of energy besides the planet's star. Or perhaps some of the star's energy penetrates the dark shroud, even though it isn't visible to human eyes. And what creates the darkness?

I freeze. Louder than everything else around me comes the sound of raspy breathing. It's directly behind me. The breaths are long and slow. The creature must be huge. And it's getting closer.

I start to turn, but something rams into my right side, nearly bowling me over. It's out of range of the Occluder before I can glimpse more than a vague mass. I turn the sonic drill toward where it disappeared, my finger hovering over the trigger. I can feel my hands quiver with fear. I strain my eyes to spot anything the moment it enters the blue bubble of my existence.

Nothing.

Is it possible that these creatures are unaware of me? Could they be heading somewhere, and I just happen to be in their path? I find it hard to believe that these two incidents were accidental. Surely the creatures can sense my presence. But why do they sweep by so sporadically?

I realize it's a stupid line of thought. I'll never know what the creatures are thinking. Why bother trying to get into their alien minds?

Deciding the ground must be cool enough, I meld a hook onto the surface and pull out the plug I cut. It's cone-shaped, about eight inches long and eight inches in diameter at the top. As soon as I hold the scanner up to the hole, it starts vibrating and the monitor flashes. It definitely detects iridium.

Placing a hook on the ground to mark my starting point, I begin another cut, this one much wider. Hopefully when I'm done, there will be iridium somewhere in the plug. It's incredible that I have to use such a crude method to try and find iridium for our sophisticated star drive. I feel like a blind cave man who's been asked to locate the buried fuel cell of a hopper.

Sweat starts to stream down my nose and cheeks despite the climate-control of my suit. My arms and legs feel weak from my nervous trembling. It's hard to hold the sonic drill steady.

I should be back to the hook by now. Did I move in a circle, or have I gone off on a tangent instead? Should I make my turn tighter? If I do, I might accidentally step on ground that I've cut. It won't do any good to change my cutting pattern at random. With that decided, I maintain my turn and keep the drill going, hoping I'm not too far off the mark.

Two steps later I see the hook. I finish the cut. A braying howl makes me jump. It sounds like it's coming from something close enough to touch. I hold the sonic drill like a rifle and pivot around, trying to spot any threat. Nothing flashes into my sphere.

Completing a full circle, I focus back on the job at hand. This plug is big enough that I can meld a hook to the center without waiting for the edges to cool. Once the hook is in place, I attach a cable, squat low like the anchor of a tug-of-war team, and pull.

The plug doesn't budge.

I wrap the cable around my hands several times for a better grip, take a deep breath, and try again. This time the plug slides up several inches, pauses, then slides a bit more. One more spurt of effort allows me to haul the plug the rest of the way out of its hole.

I run the scanner over the wide cone of rock. It flashes, indicating the presence of iridium. However, if I'm reading the monitor correctly, it doesn't look like there's much. I scan the hole. It flashes urgently, a dark blue amidst the ghostly lighter blue of the surroundings. There's definitely more iridium down there, and it appears to be close. The next plug should be what I need.

I get to work on the same hole, cutting as deep as I dare. If I dig too deep, the plug will be too heavy for me to pull out. Since I have the edge of my second cut as a reference point, this cut goes much quicker. Soon I have a new plug, hollow at the top, solid the last two-thirds of the way down to its point. It looks like a golf tee left by some absent-minded giant.

Now for the moment of truth. I scan the length of rock. The monitor flashes rapidly. I won't be able to tell for certain until I get back into the light of the lander, but I'm confident there's iridium in this core of rock.

The plug is obviously too big to fit in my backpack. I'm going to have to figure out another way to move it. After a bit of thinking, I fashion a harness out of the cable, slip it across my chest under my armpits, and begin hauling.

It's grueling work. The plug doesn't slide easily; it keeps getting caught on protrusions in the ground. I follow my lifeline back, hoping with each step that I'll catch sight of the lander.

That's when it happens.

There's a moment's warning – a flash of shadow in the corner of my eye. The next thing I know, I'm on the ground. Something heavy is on top of me, claws and fangs tearing at my spacesuit. All of the hoots and howls, snarls and growls seem to grow in intensity, as if a group of spectators is urging my attacker on. Fear crashes through my body, my heart thumps painfully in my chest. I can feel death approaching.

It's awful. I'm all alone. No one even knows I'm in trouble. I scream, even though I know it won't do any good. It's almost certainly futile to fight. The beast outweighs me, and I can feel from its muscles that it is far more powerful than me.

Adrenaline surges through my veins. I start flailing away with the ferocity of pure terror, kicking, punching, rolling, doing anything I can to get away, but knowing that even if I do rise to my feet, the iridium plug will make it easy for the creature to catch me again.

Pain scorches through my back, and more pain erupts along my left leg. I know I'm doomed, but I'm determined to fight for as long as I possibly can. I see Mom's face before me. The sight of her gentle smile gives me renewed strength. I don't want to let her down.

There's a flash to my right, as if something else has entered my blue sphere of light. Has another creature come to play tug-of-war with my body? I shout out, but I'm so focused on my opponent I'm not sure if words come out, or only nonsense.

The fight becomes my entire universe: teeth, claws, body slams, screeches, snarls. Nothing else exists. And suddenly, even the fight ceases to exist. I slip to blackness.

CHAPTER 17

Fire and Ice

A raging inferno of agony. This is all I know. I am unaware of my surroundings, or even who I am. I don't know anything that has happened before this point in my life. All is pain. I'm not even sure how I know words like pain and life. The blazing furnace consumes me, and I'm met by darkness once again.

———

The first thing I am aware of is a faint glow tingeing the edge of my darkness. It doesn't seem to have a color. Or perhaps it's a mixture of many colors. I can't really tell. I just know there is something invading my blackness, like water seeping through cracks in a wall.

Next is the pain: a dull ache that seems to come from everywhere. The glimmer of light grows, and so does the pain. I realize my eyelids are cracked open – that's where the light is coming from. But where am I?

My mind turns over the puzzle slowly, as if my brain is set at half-speed. What has happened? Why is my body so sore? Why is the light so surprising?

For a while, no answers come. Everything is blank. I have no memories of what has happened, no clues to latch onto. After a long stretch where my memory bank remains bare, an image sputters to life, forming a familiar face, and then a few more images wander through my mind: I catch a glimpse of Kartak in a spacesuit, helping me load up with tools. A hatch opens, and… darkness.

The black planet.

It all comes rushing back to me: my mission to find iridium; cutting the plugs; hauling the chunk of rock; getting attacked. I don't remember much about the fight. How did I possibly survive? And again, the question presents itself: where am I?

I open my eyes fully. A rainbow of colors greets me. The pain in my head intensifies, rising to a sharp spear in the middle of my forehead. My eyes close reflexively.

The pain slowly eases off.

It's the light. It's too bright. The problem is, I won't figure anything out with my eyes closed. I have to endure the pain.

My eyes flutter open again. The pain is still there. So is the rainbow. I'm obviously no longer on the dark planet. Everything is hazy. I can't make out any details in my surroundings.

As my eyes slowly adjust, I see walls, a ceiling, and past the ends of my toes (I'm lying on my back on some kind of cot or bed) I see the lander. I must be aboard the *Aurora*! Somehow, we made it back. I say we, because there is no way I could have returned on my own. Kartak must be here somewhere. And, of course, everyone else as well.

I roll my head to the left. My neck is so stiff, I'm half-surprised it doesn't creak like rusted hinges. I see only bare walls. I crank my head to the right. Another cot is set up a few yards away. On it I see a sleeping form. Kartak. I hear a great deal of huffing and puffing, followed by heavy footsteps. Only one person would make that much noise.

I lift my head off the cot and gaze past my feet. A large bulge appears in the lander's exterior hatchway. The bulge grows larger, and then legs, arms, and a head full of wild hair appear. Wiggs. The sight of him brings a smile to my face, and I almost forget my pain. Almost.

"Hey th…" I start to say. It comes out as a dry croak. I clear my throat and try again. "Hey there." This time my voice works a little better.

"Hey Sean, you're awake! That's great to see. You really had me worried there!"

"Is there water?" I ask. My throat feels like it's experiencing a desert drought.

"Of course, right away!" Wiggs replies. He does a U-turn and disappears back into the lander. The big guy returns a minute or so later with a glass of water.

I manage to prop myself part-way up onto my right forearm and accept the cup from him. My hand trembles visibly, sloshing water onto my wrist. I take a couple of sips. The water feels cool and revitalizing as it streams down my throat.

Suddenly, my right arm collapses. I spill the rest of the water onto the deck. What a complete wimp! I can't even hold myself up for more than a few seconds.

"Here, I'll take that," Wiggs says, scooping the glass from my shaking hand. "Do you want more?"

"In a while," I say, trying to calm the tremors in my body. "First I want to know what happened. How did Kartak find me? How did he deal with the beasts?"

"He was able to tell me most of it," Wiggs says.

"Most of it?" I say. "Why? What happened to him?"

"He was injured as well," Wiggs explains. "With the state he's in, I don't know how he managed to fly the lander, much less find the *Aurora* and land."

"Is he going to be alright?" I ask, anxiety creeping through my body. "Well, will he?" I demand after Wiggs hesitates.

"I think so," he replies. "I've taken care of his wounds, just like I've taken care of yours."

He looks concerned, and I don't have to ask why. The images of Roberts' wounds are still too fresh in my mind. It looked like he was almost completely recovered. And then he was dead. Will that happen to me? The thought makes my body tremble even more violently. The pain doubles. I start to gasp for air…

Take a deep breath. Relax. Worrying won't do me any good. It takes a few moments, but I'm able to calm my body. The trembles turn into small tremors. I can breathe normally. "Just tell me what happened," I say out loud.

"He had an uneasy feeling, so he grabbed your lifeline and followed it out. Soon he heard yelling. You were delirious. Suddenly, the darkness disappeared, replaced by the blue glow of the Occluder. You were slumped on the ground. A large creature was pawing at you.

"He didn't have time to bring the repeater up before the creature whirled on him. He smashed the thing several times with the butt of the repeater. At first this gave him the advantage, but the beast recovered and struck him four or five times with its paws. Kartak went in close to prevent the creature from taking swings at him. He grappled with it for a while, trying to find a vulnerable spot.

"The creature managed to knock him away. Kartak slid outside the Occluder's influence for a moment. He got the repeater into position and rolled back into the blue illumination.

"The beast loomed directly over him, ready to tear into his face shield with its fangs," Wiggs continues after a short, dramatic pause. "He fired several times into the creature's mouth. At first it didn't seem to have any effect. He changed his aim and fired into the main mass of its body. The beast stumbled and fell backward, almost landing on top of you. As it was, it landed on the tether you used to drag the iridium. With you on one side, and the iridium chunk on the other, he couldn't roll the creature off the cable, so he had to figure out a way to work the cable out from under the creature. It took Kartak a while to free it.

"I don't know how, but he managed to drag you and the iridium back to the lander. He couldn't do a complete decontamination because of the rends in your suits. He did the best he could, then somehow found his way back here."

Wiggs pauses and strokes his goatee. I've been imagining the scene as Wiggs describes it. Kartak continues to amaze me. And I don't have to ask how Wiggs is able to describe the events in such detail: when Kartak tells a story, he does a very thorough job of it.

"The captain was beside himself when we discovered that your suits were breached. He immediately ordered the landing bay to be sealed back up. I volunteered to stay in here and care for you. For a moment I thought the captain would deny the request. But he simply had the hatch sealed while I gathered supplies, and then opened it just long enough for me to squeeze through. I thought he was going to close it on my back hair, he made it so tight."

I chuckle at the description. "Thanks for all you've done," I say. My mind seems to be fading. I yawn, my eyelids close, and I slip into a slumber.

———

I'm burning. I'm freezing. My body can't decide. It cycles between fire and ice. Pain ripples through my skull, ebbs and flows like a tide through my back and down my legs. My fingers scratch at my spine and come away feeling slick; Wiggs has slathered me with ointment again. The cot I'm on seems to tilt forward and backward, and the landing bay walls whirl around in a wild dance.

I'm going crazy. That's the only explanation for it. Either that, or I'm going to die. Which would I prefer? Right now I don't know.

A sharp ache shoots through my skull. It feels like someone is driving an ax through my forehead. I reach both hands up and hold it, trying to drive the demons from my mind.

Tulip people float around me, changing colors like chameleon fireworks. They seem overjoyed. I glide among them without a spacesuit. The air smells like peppermint. Suddenly, I realize I can understand everything they are communicating. They talk about eating, and rain, and summer glides through gardens.

I'm caught up in their passion and a fierce joy envelops me. This is where I want to be. It is paradise.

An abrupt darkness blankets everything. Hearing is the only sense that works: howls, groans, growls. No! Not this! The blackness is like a beast coming to devour me. I can't handle it, I must escape!

Then I realize it isn't completely black. There is a faint rainbow-colored glow. My eyes adjust, and in a rush I see a fanged face looming over me. I try to scoot back, but I seem to be caught in some kind of goo. I want to close my eyes, but they seem to be stuck open. The creature reaches out an enormous paw…

Tap. Tap tap tap on my forearm. It's the mother sloth-bear! All tension drains away. The darkness flees, and I'm held in her warm embrace. I lay my cheek against her soft fur, letting minutes slip by. I'm safe. Nothing can hurt me. I'm no longer too hot or too cold. My body feels just right. I see Mom's face just beyond the sloth-bear. She sings me a lullaby…

The fevers and chills pass. The hallucinations fade with them. The deck no longer pitches; the walls have ceased their crazy twirls. There is no pain. The only things I feel right now are hunger and thirst.

———

I'm jarred awake by a rhythmic thumping, like the steam locomotives from the holo-movies I used to watch. I gaze around, searching for the source. Everything is blurry. It's hard to make anything out. What has happened to my eyes? What is making that annoying noise?

Then I identify it: my heartbeat. It's as if my heart is pounding molten metal into a sword. The feverish feeling returns. Is this normal?

I barely finish the thought when my muscles go berserk. I feel my body thrash around on the cot. I have no control over it. Panic seizes me, and my heart thumps even louder. The metal legs of the cot start to rattle against the deck plating. Any second now, it's going to tip over and I'll be thrown to the cold, hard floor.

Suddenly, I see Wiggs rush toward me – I've never seen the big guy move so fast! He forces my clenched jaws open and sprays something into my mouth. Either it doesn't have any flavor, or the spasms in my muscles are overriding all other sensations.

Slowly, I feel the large jerky movements of my body become less frequent. After a while they also diminish in intensity, until they become mild tremors. And finally, my muscles relax completely. My body and mind are exhausted. My eyes slip shut, and I'm drawn back into the blackness of the abyss.

CHAPTER 18

Rafiki's Plight

Kartak and I are both fine. Our wounds have scabbed over, and the smaller ones have already disappeared. Neither of us has had a fever for over two days. Nothing unusual is happening to our bodies.

But the captain still won't let us out of the landing bay.

It's frustrating. We still have the iridium in here. The ship needs it. We were running low before I went down to the dark planet. The *Aurora* must be almost out by now. And we still need to purify what we can from the chunk I dug up.

But the captain won't let us out.

I flip through the menu on my graphic pad. I have already spent too much time studying. If I have to read one more history text, I'll probably scream. The pad only has a couple of simple games that are boring. What can I do?

Something suddenly catches my eye: the tulip people's language. The last time I was in quarantine, I studied it to pass the time. I decide to resume my attempt to learn the language.

When in the orange strip of light, a color shift to amethyst means water. However, if the ending color is just slightly lighter, it appears to be some kind of verb (the computer isn't sure exactly what).

Studying the tiny differences of the color shifts reminds me of the sloth-bears' tapping language. You have to be very precise with both languages, otherwise you will say something completely different from what you intend. Communication is challenging enough when everyone speaks the same language. Slight changes in tone or body language, sarcasm, idioms, and dialects all color the meaning of what people say (not to mention people who only say half of what they're thinking, or those who say the complete opposite of what they mean). It makes things so confusing! And here are new languages created by alien minds who think alien thoughts. It's amazing we were able to communicate with them at all!

I return my attention to the tulip people's language. The different color combinations make my head spin: yellow to periwinkle, violet to rust, and on and on. I keep at it for close to an hour before I have to rest my eyes.

Easing back onto my cot, I close my eyes and try to imagine what Rafiki is doing. Considering how he has been behaving recently, he's probably sleeping. Still, I wish he was with me now. Even asleep he would be some moral support.

A sudden jolt goes through my mind. Wiggs is supposed to be feeding Rafiki. But Wiggs is stuck in here with us. Rafiki hasn't been fed for several days! Has he starved to death?

Frantic, I sit up. "Wiggs!" I shout. My mind is racing, trying to think of a way to escape quarantine.

Wiggs waddles quickly from the lander. "What's bothering you?" he asks, obviously hearing the anxiety in my voice.

"Rafiki doesn't have any food. He's going to starve to death!"

"Oh, that," he says, sounding relieved. How can he take it so calmly? Rafiki might be dying – "I left him a dozen large chunks of meat, and some veggies from hydroponics. As long as we get out of here in the next day or two, he should be fine."

This doesn't make me feel much better. The way the captain is treating us, it could be another week before we're allowed out. And is Wiggs really sure Rafiki has enough food?

I get up and stalk toward the landing bay hatch. It's still tightly sealed, as expected. I consider trying different combinations on the keypad. Would it be possible to guess the captain's code? How many figures is it? How many of those are letters, how many are numbers, and how many are symbols? There are just too many possibilities. I couldn't accidentally stumble upon it, even if I spent years trying. Giving up on the idea, I nose around, trying to find another way to open the hatch. No luck.

I walk around the landing bay, my nervous energy making it impossible to sit down. I have already inspected every inch of the hangar multiple times, but I scrutinize it again. I'm scanning a ventilation screen (it looks small, but perhaps if I twisted and turned…) when I suddenly become aware of a click and a hum behind me. It takes my brain a moment to register the sounds, and another moment before I turn to see their source. I feel my eyes widen in surprise. The inner hatch. It's opening!

"Kartak, Wiggs, they're letting us out!" I yell as I jog to the hatchway.

Everyone is assembled outside: the captain, Johnson, Marcum, Sharden, Hollins, Waph… Then I realize that *not* everyone is here. My dad isn't. I've been cooped up all this time, and he doesn't even think it's important enough to come when I get released.

Wiggs comes chugging up behind me. "It's about time," he says, cutting into my thoughts. "We're running out of food."

"And the ship's running out of iridium," Kartak growls. He's used to action; quarantine might have been even tougher on him than it was on me.

"Well, we had to make sure," the captain snaps, obviously irritated that we would question his decision to quarantine us for so long. "You saw what happened to Roberts. Do you want that to happen to everyone on board?"

"Of course not," Kartak snarls, fixing the captain with a glare.

This is getting out of hand. Kartak is heading for trouble. I don't want that to happen. We need a change of subject…

"Where's my dad?" I ask into the tense silence. This is the first thing that pops into my head; it makes my own anger return at his absence.

"He's in the brig," Waph says quietly.

I stand for a moment in complete shock. "The… the brig?" I manage to get out, not certain I've heard correctly.

"That's right, the brig," the captain thunders, spittle spraying the deck around him. He looks half-crazed. "He tried to release you without my permission. I can't have people making their own decisions when the safety of the ship is at stake. A ship has to have discipline!"

"You put him in the brig because he tried to help us?" I sputter. The resentment I felt toward Dad is instantly redirected at a new target. "That's the stup –"

"Sean!" Kartak cuts in, placing a hand on my shoulder. "We need to get the iridium purified. Come help me with it."

Anger simmers in my chest. Kartak doesn't need my help. There are plenty of other people around who can help him just as easily as I can. Once more I feel as if there's a beast in me; it's pulling at its chain, eager to attack.

I'm just about to get in the captain's face and scream about his stupidity when Kartak tightens his grip on my shoulder. He wheels me around and forces me toward the lander.

"Let me go," I say through clenched teeth, fighting against him. I almost slip away, but he grabs my other shoulder. With both hands gripping me, his hold is as secure as a steel vice.

"Calm down, Sean," he says calmly. "You won't help your father by fighting the captain. We'll get the captain to release him, but we must do it when we are calm. And more importantly, when *he* is calm.

I want to tear away from his grip, I want to argue, but it's useless. We have reached the lander, and his grip is as firm as ever. Kartak propels me through the open airlock and into the main hold.

He spins me around and looks me straight in the eye. "Now if I let you go, will you act sensibly?"

Will I act sensibly. These words make me feel like an idiot. I'm angry at the captain because of how completely foolish he is, to lock my dad away. Now Kartak's words have helped me realize just how foolish I'm acting. I gaze at the deck, trying to hide my face. It must be as red as a cardinal right now… at least, it would be in a world where cardinals are still red.

Evidently, Kartak feels my muscles relax; he releases me, even though I haven't answered him out loud. "Here you go," he says, handing me the irregular chunk of iridium. I give a grunt as the plug of ore pushes heavily against my chest. "Take it to the incinerator. I'll be there in a minute."

I nod. The iridium is blocking my view. Turning, I tap around carefully with my foot. Soon I feel the ridge where the lander's airlock seals shut, and step down to the landing bay deck. The others are still crowded by the bay door. I start to push my way through when I spot Wiggs deep in conversation with Waph. The sight of the big guy trigger's my brain. Rafiki! Is he on the edge of starvation? I have to get to him!

I make the trip to the incinerator in record time.

I heave the iridium chunk onto a bench. It starts to tip over. I quickly catch it before it topples completely off. Turning the chunk, I settle it back down onto the bench and watch for a few seconds. Once I'm certain that it's staying put, I turn on my heel and rush out the door. Kartak is still halfway down the corridor.

"There's something I need to check on," I call to him, then jog toward my quarters without waiting for an answer. My stomach feels funny. I keep picturing Rafiki lying on the floor, wheezing out his final breaths. The ship seems twice as big as normal…

Finally, I come to a halt outside the hatch to my room. I hit the sensor plate. The door whooshes to the side. My eyes frantically scan the room before it fully opens. He's not on the bed, or under the desk. He isn't anywhere on the open floor space. I duck my head under the bed… nothing. There's only one last place I can think of.

I rush to the bathroom cubicle. Inside I spot a few small chunks of gristle and random bits of vegetables, but no Rafiki. Where could he be? Did he somehow escape from my cabin? Did someone take him?

I sit heavily on my bunk. Frantic thoughts rush through my mind. Rafiki must think I've abandoned him. He needed me and I wasn't here. Now he's disappeared.

Mom once told me that cats often sneak off and find a quiet place when they are nearing the end of their life. Perhaps so they can die in peace. Is this what Rafiki has done? Could he have gotten a ventilation cover open?

I heave a big sigh, uncertain what to do. Just as I exhale, something catches my eye. There is some kind of blob in the far corner that I've never seen before. Bewildered, I wander over to investigate. The blob is ovoid. Its surface looks almost like it's been woven together from narrow strips of seaweed. Should I touch it? Could there be some poison, or something else dangerous on it? Could there be something dangerous *in* it?

This thought seems to trigger something in my brain. I suddenly know what the object is. There isn't a doubt in my mind. Rafiki has made a cocoon. His species must go through some sort of metamorphosis. That's why he's been eating so much, and why he's been so sluggish lately! He has been preparing for this.

I return to my bunk and slump down. How long will he be in the cocoon? What will he look like when he emerges? These thoughts flit through my mind. However, my curiosity is overridden by another emotion: loneliness. Rafiki is the closest thing I have to a real friend. Our food supply is better. Our water supply is better, and now we have iridium. But we still aren't any closer to finding our way home. I could be stuck on this stupid starship for several more months, if not years.

And now, I won't even have Rafiki to keep me company on the journey.

A. A. Akibibi

172

About the Author

A. A. Akibibi is the pen name for Michael Jonathan (Jon) Megahan. Jon grew up as a missionary kid in Tanzania, East Africa. He attended an international boarding school, living and interacting with people from many different cultures.

Jon currently teaches upper elementary and middle school in rural Minnesota. He enjoys volleyball, disc golf, board games, and Minnesota summers.

Thanks for reading! If you enjoyed this story, please consider telling other people about it. Word of mouth recommendations are important for authors who are just starting out.

Look for book three, currently titled Splendid Light, to be released in the spring or early summer of 2024.

For more information, including the release date for the final book of the trilogy, follow Jon on Instagram: aaakibibi

9 798985 681215